CONTACT

"Good lord," came Doctor Salik's voice.

Commander Adama crossed the control room to the short corridor the doctor had entered a moment before. "What is it?"

"I've found them," he said, coming back toward the commander.

He led him down the metal hallway into another room. Built into its floor were two rows of glass boxes, each of which held a body. There were six in all.

Dropping to his knees before the nearest box, Doctor Salik stared into it. "This is how they've journeyed across space."

Berkley Battlestar Galactica Books

BATTLESTAR GALACTICA
by Glen A. Larson and Robert Thurston

BATTLESTAR GALACTICA 2: THE CYLON DEATH MACHINE
by Glen A. Larson and Robert Thurston

BATTLESTAR GALACTICA 3: THE TOMBS OF KOBOL
by Glen A. Larson and Robert Thurston

BATTLESTAR GALACTICA 4: THE YOUNG WARRIORS
by Glen A. Larson and Robert Thurston

BATTLESTAR GALACTICA 5: GALACTICA DISCOVERS EARTH
by Glen A. Larson and Michael Resnick

BATTLESTAR GALACTICA 6: THE LIVING LEGEND
by Glen A. Larson and Nicholas Yermakov

BATTLESTAR GALACTICA 7: WAR OF THE GODS
by Glen A. Larson and Nicholas Yermakov

BATTLESTAR GALACTICA 8: GREETINGS FROM EARTH
by Glen A. Larson and Ron Goulart

BattlestaR GALACTICA 8

GREETINGS FROM EARTH

Novel by Glen A. Larson and Ron Goulart
Based on the Universal Television Series
"BATTLESTAR GALACTICA"
Created by Glen A. Larson
Adapted from the episode
"Greetings from Earth"
Written by Glen A. Larson

BERKLEY BOOKS, NEW YORK

BATTLESTAR GALACTICA 8:
GREETINGS FROM EARTH

A Berkley Book/published by arrangement with
MCA PUBLISHING, a Division of MCA Communications, Inc.

PRINTING HISTORY
Berkley edition/June 1983

ISBN: 0-425-06047-0

A BERKLEY BOOK ® TM 757,375
Berkley Books are published by Berkley Publishing Corporation,
200 Madison Avenue, New York, N.Y. 10016.
The name "Berkley" and the stylized "B" with design
are trademarks belonging to Berkley Publishing Corporation.
PRINTED IN THE UNITED STATES OF AMERICA

BATTLESTAR GALACTICA 8: GREETINGS FROM EARTH

CHAPTER ONE

He was asleep when the discovery was first made.

He was slouching in the cockpit of his small, sleek, long-range viper ship. A dead cigar dangled from between two fingers of his right hand and there was a scatter of ashes dusting the toe of one of his boots. Beyond the window of the cockpit stretched the endless dark silence of space.

All at once a tiny red bulb of light began to blink urgently on the control panel and a rude buzzing noise filled the small cockpit.

Lieutenant Starbuck straightened up, blinking. "Okay, okay," he mumbled at the dash panel. "Calm down." He stuck the cigar between his even teeth and scowled at the timedial. "Hey, you weren't supposed to wake me up for another hour yet. I'm on a sleep period and—"

"Starbuck, old buddy?"

1

A familiar voice came knifing out of one of the speaker grids.

Brushing back his straw-colored hair, Starbuck inquired, "Are you the one who caused me to be awakened out of a well-deserved snooze, Apollo?"

"That I am," replied Apollo.

"Been missing my pithy conversation?"

"Listen, shake the gunk out of your brain and act awake. Okay?"

"I'm fresh as a daisy," Starbuck assured him as he relit his stogie. "Proceed."

"I'm roughly fifty sectares ahead of you and—"

"Gee, looks like you'll beat me to the finish line and win the gold trophy."

"Quit clowning and pay attention, damn it. Something's starting to show up on my scanners."

Frowning, Starbuck asked, "Like what?"

"Think it's a ship."

"Not a Cylon craft?" Starbuck stiffened in his seat and stared out the cockpit window. "We haven't run into one of those bastards in one hell of a long—"

"Nope, this isn't a Cylon craft, good buddy. Far as I can tell . . . well, I'm getting a better look at it as we're talking and . . . this thing isn't exactly like anything I've run up against before."

Starbuck's left eye narrowed. "You sound, which is odd for a lad who's about six degrees cooler than an ice cube, excited," he said.

"I guess I am," Captain Apollo admitted. "Can you catch up with me? Quick."

"If not quicker," said Starbuck.

The *Galactica* moved majestically through space, an immense yet slim-lined multi-level vehicle. The greatest fighting ship of the Colonial Fleet, the huge battlestar was a self-contained world housing thousands. And the fate of those thousands, their ultimate destiny, was in the hands of the ship's commander.

Commander Adama was thinking of that as he sat in his quarters aboard the *Galactica,* one powerful arm resting on his metallic desk. "What was that?" he said, turning toward the man sitting in one of the visitors' chairs.

"I was remarking that your mind seemed to be elsewhere," said Colonel Tigh, smiling thinly. His right hand fidgeted, as though he was anxious to jot something down.

"Quite probably it is. Forgive me." The grey-haired man rose up and walked to the room's large oval view window. "Somewhere out there is an answer."

"Quite a few answers, no doubt." Tigh cleared his throat. "But the problem, as I see it, is—"

"The only problem you ought to be worrying about, Colonel, is your impatience."

"Impatience isn't a problem, it's an asset." He leaned forward in his chair, fingers rubbing together. "If you've read any of my recent reports on—"

"I've read, and savored, them."

"Then you know there is considerable concern, not only here aboard the *Galactica,* but in the other ships as well that—"

"By the good graces of the Lords of Kobol, the *Galactica* continues to lead her flock of survivors," cut in the deep-voiced commander. He gazed out at the vast dark emptiness they were traveling through. "We are moving toward co-ordinates given us by those great white lights that vanished as inexplicably as they appeared."

"Some fear that—"

"I'm inclined to go along with those who feel the

lights were from starships, craft from Earth. That gives us hope, since it seems to indicate that on Earth there is a highly developed technology and that if we can reach there—"

"If," said Tigh.

"Right now our long-range scouts are on patrol." Adama faced his restless visitor. "Watching for signs that might—"

"I have," said Colonel Tigh, standing, "considerable respect for your son, Captain Apollo. I know he's out there, piloting one of the scouting vipers, doing the best he can." He paused to cough into his hand. "But Lieutenant Starbuck's out there too, and you know what a hothead he is."

"Starbuck's pulled us out of quite a few rough places," said the commander as he strode back to his desk. "Admittedly he has a tendency to be flippant at inappropriate times. He's too fond of gambling and taking risks, yet I still have a good deal of faith in him."

Tigh glanced at a wall timedial. "I'm afraid I have an appointment elsewhere. If you'll excuse me, Commander?"

"Yes, get on with whatever you have to do."

Stopping at the doorway, Tigh said, "The rest of what I wanted to discuss with you, Commander Adama, I can put in a memo."

"I'm sure you can," said Adama, a faint smile touching his face.

Starbuck saw it too.

"I'll be damned," he said.

"What do you make of it?" inquired Apollo.

Their two viper ships were flying in tandem.

Moving through space toward them was a large, blocky craft. Its design and markings were unfamiliar.

Starbuck's forehead wrinkled. "You been able to get any response out of her?"

"Nary a word."

Starbuck rested his unlit cigar on the panel and punched some buttons. After a few seconds he nodded. "My scanners confirm what yours indicated," he said, after checking the readout. "This thing is a sublight vehicle. And it contains six—count 'em, six—life forms."

"But we don't know exactly what sort of critters are aboard."

"I'm betting they're humanoid," said Starbuck. "People pretty much like us and probably hailing from Earth."

"That's not confirmed yet, good buddy."

"My gut confirms it," Starbuck told him impatiently. "We've come millions of microns, searching for a contact like this. And here 'tis."

"Maybe," said Captain Apollo.

"Stay where you are." Starbuck suddenly kicked in his turbos and went shooting away from the side of the other viper.

He went zooming toward the strange and unfamiliar silvery space craft. Slowing again, he commenced flying a series of slow, expert loops around the ship.

He scrutinized the ship's underbelly, and came close enough to get a good look at the cockpit area. There were no signs of life. The cockpit was unmanned.

"Ease off," advised the voice of Apollo. "We don't want to scare these folks out of their wits, you know."

"I'm not going to unsettle them any," promised Starbuck. "Don't fret. You keep forgetting how personable I am. Remember when we met those paranurses from the—"

"Suppose the people aboard this ship are from Earth? It's highly possible they've never encountered anyone from beyond their own planet before," said Apollo.

"Which means they may just be inclined to attack any hotshot viper pilot, no matter how personable he is, who comes buzzing too—"

"C'mon, use that brilliant though diminutive brain of yours," urged Starbuck as he flew one more lazy circle around the larger ship. "Nobody inside this mysterious crate is going to do anything to me."

"It's not a derelict, Starbuck. The thing's moving under its own power and we know that six life forms are aboard. Life forms, not corpses."

Starbuck was frowning over another scanner readout. "Speaking of power, old chum, my scanners don't indicate the presence of either Corrilax or Lazon."

"That means they must be using some other form of explosive material."

"Which is another good indication they're from someplace different, someplace like Earth."

"Possibly, good buddy, but—"

"Look, they aren't responding to us." Starbuck was now flying a course parallel to that of the mystery ship. "You know what I think?"

"Something devious."

"The folks inside this crate are either in big trouble or they're in some sort of suspended state."

"Yep, that could well be," acknowledged Apollo. "Possibly we ought just to leave them to continue on their set course. No need to—"

"Are you daffy? These are, I'm damn near certain, Earth people," said Starbuck. "After all our searching and hunting, we are on the brink of making a contact."

"Just exactly how do we make this contact? If they're all in deepsleep or—"

"Obviously we've got to wake 'em up."

Apollo said, "That might mean exceeding our—"

"It doesn't. Damn it, we're on a scouting mission and

we've made us a discovery," said Starbuck, sticking the dead cigar back between his teeth. "If I was given to fancy lingo, I'd dub this discovery both monumental and stupendous. Even nifty."

"So?"

"So right now I'm going to drop a parasite control box onto the side of this baby here," announced Starbuck as he began easing his craft closer to the larger space craft. "Then we will guide her right back to the docking bay on the *Galactica*. Then we can find out exactly who and what's inside this little surprise package. Okay?"

After a few seconds Apollo replied, "Sure, okay."

CHAPTER TWO

Commander Adama came striding into the control center, the bridge, of the *Galactica*. He halted, scanning the large room and noting that several crewmen and crew-women were not at their regular posts. Instead they were either clustered at the vast view window or around the communication screen that was linked with Captain Apollo's returning viper.

"Colonel Tigh," Adama asked, "what's the meaning of this laxness?"

Tigh was standing near the entryway, gazing out at the starfield beyond their ship. "I took it upon myself to allow a certain laxity, Commander," he replied as he faced the wide-shouldered, grey-haired Adama.

Adama said, "Isn't this the very sort of behavior you usually dictate memos about? Crew neglecting assigned duties, confusion rampant on the bridge."

"This is an unusual situation," the colonel explained,

rubbing his hands together. "Captain Apollo has communicated the very gratifying news that he and Lieutenant Starbuck have discovered an Earth ship and are
escorting it back here to us."

"A possible Earth ship," corrected Adama.

"I'm certain the vehicle will prove to be outward bound
from the planet Earth," said Tigh. "Naturally, everyone
is extremely elated and they're anxious for a glimpse of
the craft and—"

"Yes, I understand." Nodding, Adama raised his voice.
"Gentlemen, ladies," he said. "I fully appreciate the
uniqueness of what may be happening. However, I must
ask you to return now to your stations. This may or may
not be our long-awaited contact with an Earth vehicle.
Whatever it is, we must proceed with maximum effi-
ciency and caution."

Murmuring, reluctant as children leaving a carnival
early, the crew members drifted back to their assigned
posts on the *Galactica* bridge.

"Thank you," Adama said to them. "Now I think I'd
better get on the unicom and address everyone, since I
have a hunch the excitement is going to be spreading
throughout the fleet."

"It already is," confirmed Tigh, following the commander to the nearest unicom pickup.

"I'd like you to take charge of seeing to it that the
designated area of the landing bay is cleared of all un-
authorized personnel. I've already alerted Doctor Salik
and his medical team to be standing by with full decontamination crew and equipment." Adama reached for the
unicom switch.

Lieutenant Jolly had his broad back turned to the nearest view window of the rec lounge. Hunched slightly, a
look of admiration on his plump face, he was gazing

across the small table at his date. "No, I think you've got a lovely name. Zixi. Sure, there's a lilt to it and—"

"You really and truly think so?" inquired the pretty auburn-haired Zixi. "Because some people are apt to—"

"Heck, don't I know what it's like to have a name jerks kid about?" he said. "I mean a tag like Jolly is open to attack from all sorts of annoying angles, you know. 'Not living up to your name today, huh?' or 'Hi, Jolly, you don't look much like your name.' or 'When's your next family reunion, so we can get our Jollys?' and so on."

The paranurse's pretty freckled nose wrinkled very slightly. "With my name it isn't so much puns and plays on words, Jolly, as it is just. . . . Well, for one thing it's sort of hard to pronounce right."

"Zixi? That's not tough at all. Nell's bells, I could write a song around your name with no troub—"

"Actually, you aren't pronouncing it exactly right either."

He straightened up, smote his broad chest with a fist. "It's not pronounced Zixi?"

"The X has more of a Z sound."

"Ah," said Lieutenant Jolly, nodding sagely. "Well, I always say, a meech by any other name would smell as—"

"What's a meech?"

"A flower. They grow wild all over several planets I've visited in my day. The thing is, they smell pretty good," the hefty lieutenant explained. "Which is why this saying came about, see. A meech by any other name would smell as sweet. It isn't what your name is, but what you are inside that counts."

"True," admitted Zixi. "But sometimes I wish my

name were Anne Marie or Dolly or even—"

"Why don't you tell me more about yourself?" suggested Jolly. "Ever since I met you at the airpong table the other night shift I've been wondering about you."

"Let's see," said Zixi, tapping the rim of her ambrosia glass. "I'm an only child. Both my mother and father have funny names, too. There's a long family tradition of—"

"What say we forget names," put in Jolly. "Or maybe I can make up a nickname for you and then—"

"People of the fleet, your attention please." Commander Adama's voice came booming out of the overhead unicom speakers.

"Something big," muttered Jolly, looking away from the young woman and up at a speaker grid.

"Rumors are spreading faster than fact about the discovery of a manned vehicle to be brought aboard the *Galactica*," continued the commander. "I must ask you all to be patient and cautious in your optimism. The incoming vessel will have to be placed in careful quarantine before we can allow anyone near it for fear of jeopardizing not only our own lives but the lives of whoever may be aboard this space craft. Bulletins on every phase of our operation will be transmitted to all of you as soon as reliable facts become available. I ask you to bear with us and be patient. Thank you."

Jolly rocked back in his chair as the commander's last words faded away. "Hey, that's darn exciting," he said, tugging at his moustache.

An excited murmur of talk was filling the lounge as the other patrons began to discuss Commander Adama's message.

Zixi said, "It may mean we'll be able to settle on Earth."

"It sure might." Jolly popped up to his feet. Then he

bent and took the young woman's hand. "I remain deeply devoted to you, Zixi. . . . Did I pronounce it okay that time around?"

"Pretty near."

"Good. Anyway, I want to scoot to the docking area right fast," he informed her. "We'll rendezvous again soon as this crisis passes." Bowing, he deposited a smacking kiss on her hand and then went trotting out.

CHAPTER THREE

Starbuck, chewing hard on the end of his latest cigar, went hurrying along the metal-walled corridor. "I'd like to see 'em try," he was saying.

Apollo, lagging a few paces behind, said, "You know damn well they won't let us anywhere near the thing until it's safely decontaminated."

"We found that ship," said Starbuck. He halted before an elevator door and gave the down button an angry push. "We hauled it back here to the *Galactica*, at great personal risk of life and limb. Hell, Apollo, it's our baby. Sort of, you know, like an orphan we found out in a storm or a stray dog we took in out of—"

"Quit, quit, you're bringing tears to my eyes," laughed Apollo.

The elevator door whooshed open and the anxious Lieutenant Starbuck dived in. "I'd dearly love to see you get exuberant about something. Here we've made a fantastic find and you—"

"People can be pleased and not flap their arms or shoot steam out of their ears."

"But that's what life is all about. Flapping your arms, jumping up and down, having a good time and showing it," said the lieutenant as the elevator cage dropped them swiftly toward the docking area where the ship they'd found had been taken. "That's how you know you're alive."

"There are other ways of telling."

The doors swished open and they saw a long corridor crowded with people. At its end two impassive security guards stood blocking the entrance to the landing bay.

Spotting Starbuck and Apollo, Lieutenant Jolly pushed his way back to them. "Hey, fellas, what gives?"

Starbuck asked him, "Are those security nitwits yonder keeping everyone out?"

"Yep, they are," complained the hefty lieutenant. "I came hustling down here from the lounge, leaving behind an absolutely striking young woman with hair the color of—"

"Spare me the details of your sordid love life, Jolly." Starbuck, using elbow and shoulder, pushed into the curious crowd.

Following in his wake, Captain Apollo cautioned, "Don't go punching anybody in the snoot, good buddy. Because I won't come visiting you in the brig."

"Hooey," observed Starbuck, his cigar tilting to a warlike angle. "All I'm after is fair play. It's an established rule of galactic salvage that the discoverer of—"

"We're not talking about derelict cargo ships."

"Stop right there, Starbuck," advised the larger of the two large guards.

Hands on hips, Starbuck scowled at the young man. "Look, try to comprehend what I am about to impart to you. Utilize every single cell of that pea-size brain of yours. I intend to—"

"No admittance."

"Listen, I'm the guy who found that damn crate," Starbuck informed him. "I've got a right to visit. . . . Quit poking me, Apollo."

Someone had tapped the feisty lieutenant on the shoulder.

"Now, as I was saying. . . ." Starbuck noticed that the guard had stiffened to attention and he decided he'd better look back over his shoulder. "Oh. . . . How do you do, Commander?"

"Fine, Lieutenant Starbuck," replied Commander Adama, who'd made his way to the door. "Allow me to personally congratulate you two for the excellent job you've done."

Grinning, Starbuck snapped his fingers. "All in a day's work, sir," he said modestly. "Now will you explain to these overzealous guardians here that I have a perfect right to—"

"I'm afraid none of us can get a closer look until Doctor Salik says it's safe," the commander said.

"Not even you?"

Adama shook his head. "Not even me."

"So what do we do?"

"We wait."

A temporary wall of tough see-through plastic stood between them and the space craft. The vehicle looked much smaller sitting in the vast landing bay.

Doctor Salik took off the headpiece of his decontamination suit and then nodded back at the ship. "It's clean," he said.

His two associates, Cassiopea and Doctor Wilker, were standing nearby.

Adama, flanked by Apollo and Starbuck, faced Salik. "What can you tell us?"

Stroking his chin, Salik leaned against a metal guard

rail. "It's possible, based on fairly unsophisticated early tests, that this craft you've brought to us is from Earth."

"Told you so." Starbuck bounced on his heels and chuckled.

"Remind me to give you something for your nerves," said Salik.

"Nerves? Hell, I'm the only one around here with any feelings." Starbuck pointed a thumb at the ship. "Everybody ought to be excited as I am, Doc, because right inside that crate yonder may be the answers to all our—"

"Perhaps," said Doctor Wilker, moving nearer to them.

"You just now said it came from Earth," said Starbuck, impatient.

"On the contrary, young man, it was my colleague who alluded to the possibility of an Earth origin for this ship," corrected Wilker. "Let me, before we proceed further, remind you that he is a medical man and I am a scientist. Our points of view, therefore, won't always match up nor—"

"Holy H. Crow," said Starbuck, waving his cigar in the air and gazing up at the fretwork high above. "Don't give us a whole darn lecture in Dumbbell Science One-A, Doc. What we—"

"Lieutenant," said the commander, "suppose you allow me to ask the initial questions."

Starbuck took a deep breath. "Okay, sorry."

Cassiopea smoothed her tunic and then sat on a stray metal drum. "Let me anticipate one of your possible questions, Commander," she offered. "We did confirm the life signs within the ship."

"Yes, that is certain," said Doctor Salik, nodding. "There are six separate entities, all alive."

"Six," said Adama, "and all alive?"

"Yes, exactly," answered Salik.

"Yet there's been no response from within the vehicle?"

"None thus far," said Salik. "I believe, however, that there is a simple explanation for that, and my associates agree."

"Partially," put in Doctor Wilker.

"You think," Adama guessed, "that these people inside, whoever they are, must be in some sort of state of suspended animation?"

"We do, yes."

"That," added Doctor Wilker, "is one possible explanation."

"We have established that none of the people inside are responding to this present situation at all," said Cassiopea. "Their life signs are all even and there have been no increases in heart rate or respiration to indicate fright, anger or even simple awareness that their flight has been interrupted."

"Has any attempt been made," asked Commander Adama, "to enter the craft?"

"I wanted your direct order first before attempting that," said Doctor Salik.

"We ought to go in at once," said Wilker. "I see no reason at all to delay further the—"

"Wait a moment," said Adama, thoughtful. "Will we be likely to upset any critical balance by violating the seals and entering the ship?"

"That is not likely," answered Salik. "We were able to penetrate the hull with a probe. The gas levels and atmosphere inside were sampled and tested."

"And you learned what?"

"There is almost zero atmosphere. There are traces of oxygen, carbon dioxide.... Certainly nothing that would sustain life as we know it."

"Since no one could survive under such conditions,"

said the commander, "we must assume that these six passengers are being cared for in a separate and isolated life support system somewhere within."

"Yes, exactly," said Doctor Salik.

"Very well." Adama locked his hands together and bowed his head for a few seconds. "Let's go into the ship."

CHAPTER FOUR

Doctor Salik crossed the threshold first, stepping into the dimly lit control room of the mystery ship. "Sufficient air from the landing bay has seeped in here," he announced. "The rest of you can come on in."

Wilker said, "I don't quite see why viper pilots should be allowed to get in the way of—"

"Listen, Doc," said Starbuck, putting his hand on the scientist's arm, "this baby is just as important to us as—"

"Doctor," said Commander Adama evenly, "these men are here at my invitation."

"Very well." After making a mock bow, Wilker stepped into the ship.

"After you, Cassie," Starbuck said to the young woman.

As soon as she entered he followed.

There was only a faint glow of light in the control

room, coming from thin panels of frosted glass along the floor line. Two of the walls were thick with dials and switches, buttons and grids. The walls and ceiling, part metal and part plastic, were pale blue and pale red. The pebbled floor was a grayish white.

Starbuck crossed to what was obviously the pilot's seat and scrutinized the controls. "Never seen anything like this before," he remarked.

"Everything seems to be functioning," Cassiopea observed.

"Doc," said Starbuck to Wilker, "your boys ought to be able to figure all these gadgets out."

"Given time, yes, certainly." Hands behind his back, he was scanning a wall. "They seem to favor a different mathematical system than we do, but once I feed some of this data into my computers I—"

"Good lord," came Doctor Salik's voice.

Commander Adama crossed the control room to the short corridor the doctor had entered a moment before. "What is it?"

"I've found them," he said, coming back toward the commander.

He led him down the metal hallway into another room. Built into its floor were two rows of glass boxes, each of which held a body. There were six in all.

Dropping to his knees before the nearest box, Doctor Salik stared into it. "This is how they've journeyed across space."

"Are they alive?" the commander asked as he knelt beside the doctor.

"This fellow certainly is," Salik answered, easing a pencil-sized instrument out of his pocket and touching it, gently, to the lid of the box. "Yes, all his vital signs register. But he's functioning at a very low level, in a sort of trance state."

"He looks to be a young man somewhere in his late twenties," said Adama, studying the sleeping face on the other side of the glass wall of the coffin.

"About that, yes."

"Some of them are just kids," said Cassiopea, who was slowly circling the built-in boxes. "This little fellow here can't be more than five or six."

"This guy's wife is sort of cute," commented Starbuck, pointing down at the slim blonde young woman who occupied the glass box next to that of the dark young man Doctor Salik was hunched over. "Not a very romantic trip for 'em, though. Laid out in see-through coffins. They should've asked their travel agent for first class accommodations instead of—"

"Hush up, good buddy," advised Apollo.

"Yes, do," seconded Wilker, who was studying the complex of wires and tubes that came snaking out of the metal walls to attach to each of the six glass coffins. "Obviously their metabolism has been lowered to its minimum for sustaining life. This support system is set to maintain that life for as long as need be."

Folding his arms, Apollo leaned against a wall. "How long have they been like this?"

Salik answered him. "Quite a long time, I'd say."

Still surveying the sleeping young woman, Starbuck said, "We have to talk with them, communicate in some way. How do we wake 'em up?"

"Very carefully," answered Salik. "If their awakening isn't handled exactly right, they'll no doubt die."

"You may be exaggerating," said Wilker.

"We've found humans," said Starbuck. "Quite probably from Earth. How soon before we can revive them and have them talk to us?"

"You can be sure our curiosity is as great, if not greater, than yours, Lieutenant," said Doctor Salik. "The revival of these half-dozen wayfarers will be accomplished as quickly as it can be done without endangering their lives."

"I'd be inclined to select one of them and start making tests at once," said Doctor Wilker. "We can start with one of the children, say. If something does go wrong, which is highly unlikely, we've only lost a—"

"You'll use none of them as guinea pigs, Doctor Wilker," said Commander Adama slowly and carefully. "Is that absolutely clear to you? Who these people are and where they're going may be critically important to our own survival. I want absolutely no chances taken."

"I certainly didn't mean to imply we'd be slipshod in—"

"Just so we understand each other." Adama turned to Salik. "Before any attempt is made to open a single one of these cases, you'll run every test possible. And then, Doctor, I want you to confer directly with me before taking any further step."

"Of course, Commander. I was intending to proceed in that manner anyway."

"Might I make a suggestion?" said Wilker. "Now that the sightseeing is over, I'd like you to leave us alone to our work." He nodded in the direction of Starbuck.

Deciding not to thumb his nose, Starbuck said, "They're all yours, Doc. For now."

CHAPTER FIVE

Excitement had spread to every part of the *Galactica,* even to the school bay of the huge battlestar, where a slightly distracted young woman was trying to conduct a class in Applied Science. She stood, not quite patiently, at the head of the domed room and watched the two dozen children in her charge. They were whispering and chattering among themselves.

"Kids," said Athena, clapping her hands, "let's settle down again and see if we can't get some work done before the period ends. Okay?"

A silence, momentary at best, settled over the children and they all gazed up at the slim, chestnut-haired young woman.

"I know most of you are aware that something special's been happening. Naturally you're interested and excited, but still we—"

"People from Earth!" spoke out a brown-haired boy

at a desk near the front of the room. "We've found people from Earth."

"Boxey, when you want to address the class, use your question indicator. Please?"

"Yesum, Athena." The boy brushed a lock of hair off his high forehead. He flipped a toggle on his desktop and a red blip of light flickered. "But that's what they found, sure enough."

"That seems the likely conclusion, although Doctor Salik and his staff aren't absolutely certain yet," said Athena. "And it's possible, therefore, that what happens in the next day or so will have an effect on each and every one of us."

Another little light flashed, at the desk of a small blonde girl.

"Yes, Loma?"

"Are there really people inside the ship that Lieutenant Starbuck brought back?"

"As far—"

"It was my father, Apollo, who found the ship and brought it here," put in Boxey. "I mean, Starbuck was along, but it was—"

"Boxey, your light. Remember?"

"Sorry, Athena. But she hadn't ought to say that it was—"

"Yes, we understand. It was Captain Apollo and Lieutenant Starbuck, while on a scouting patrol, who found this mysterious ship and brought it back to us," said Athena. "Now, did you have a question, Loma?"

The little girl made a face at the nearby Boxey. "Every time I try to ask something, he hollers at me."

"Boxey didn't mean to interrupt you, Loma. And he's sorry."

"Yeah, sure," said Boxey. "I'm sorry. But it was my dad as much as—"

"Boxey."

"Excuse me," the boy said.

"Loma?"

"I wanted to know if there were really people in the ship?"

"There are, yes."

Another light flashed.

"Yes, Wally?"

A black boy asked, "What kind of people? Are they monsters or what?"

The teacher smiled. "They appear to be very much like us, so I guess we can't call them monsters."

Loma asked, "Why don't the people come out?"

"There are several reasons. The main one being that they're apparently in a state of suspended animation," answered Athena. "Do you know what that means? Boxey?"

His light had been flashing. "Means they're sort of like taking a nap. Only one hell of a . . . excuse me. One awful long one."

Wally's light blinked. "Why are they asleep? Wouldn't you want to stay awake on a trip, so you could see everything?"

Athena said, "Well, on a very long trip, when you're traveling immense distances, you have to sleep. In fact, you have to be put in a state where your body is slowed down. That way you don't age much."

"Otherwise," said Boxey, "everybody'd get to their destination and be old. A bunch of old people wouldn't do much good on a rough—"

"Boxey, there are many benefits that come with age. One of which is patience and tolerance."

"I flashed my light that time," he told her.

Wally asked, "Where are they going to?"

"We don't know that yet."

Loma said, "Maybe they'll never get there now. On account of we stopped them. Was that right to do?"

Athena rubbed her palm with the fingers of her other hand. "We think it was, since these people may be able to tell us things that are very important to us."

"They're going to feel funny," said the little girl. "Waking up and they aren't where they thought they were."

"Maybe they won't wake up," said Boxey.

Athena gave him a frowning look. "What do you mean by that, Boxey?"

"Well, Doctor Wilker may make a mistake and they'll all die before he can get them out of their coffins."

"Why are they in coffins?" asked a lanky boy near the rear of the room.

"You said they weren't dead," Loma said. "If they're alive how come they're in coffins then?"

"Boxey was using a figure of speech," said the young woman. "As I understand it, the space travelers are resting in glass cubicles."

"When will they wake up?" another child wanted to know.

"As soon as it can be safely done," answered Athena.

"Sooner if Doc Wilker messes up," said Boxey.

"Young man, it really isn't polite to be so critical of the doctor."

"He's an arrogant nitwit," said Boxey. "I know, because I heard my father say so. And Lieutenant Starbuck agreed. He said Wilker was a cold fish, too, Starbuck did. I'm not exactly sure what—"

"You mustn't pay attention to most of what Lieutenant Starbuck says," the teacher cautioned.

Loma's light flashed again. "What do you think the Earth people will have to tell us?"

Athena answered, "I really am not sure."

She found him in a long blank-walled corridor. "Apollo," called Athena.

The captain had been strolling purposefully along a few yards ahead of her. He halted, turned around and smiled. "Ah, my favorite schoolmarm and sister."

Instead of returning his smile, the young woman frowned. "I want to talk to you."

"Something about Boxey?" He rested one palm flat against the metal wall. "Last report I had from him, he was doing okay in everything except deport—".

"It's about you as much as it is about Boxey," she said.

"I really didn't help him with that last math paper, no matter what he says."

"It's about the Earth people."

"Possible Earth people," he corrected.

"The children are quite excited about what's happening," she went on, "and naturally we've been discussing the whole thing in class."

"Just about everybody aboard the *Galactica* is excited. This is a big event."

Athena said, "That's why I don't want your negative attitude upsetting the kids."

"Negative? Starbuck and I are the ones who spotted the ship and brought it home. Maybe I don't jump up and down and wave a cigar like Starbuck does, but I assure you, Athena, I'm just as—"

"I can understand your talking freely in front of Boxey, although I might not raise a child of mine that way," she said. "The thing is, Apollo, the boy isn't old enough or sophisticated enough to know when you two are maybe kidding. And sometimes you voice opinions in front of him that should be kept to yourselves."

"You sound like you're accusing me of telling him dirty stories."

"He was repeating in class some nasty remarks you and Starbuck made about Doctor Wilker."

Apollo gave a short laugh. "Come on, Athena," he said. "I'm not going to pretend that I think Wilker isn't a cold-blooded, officious son of a—"

"I'm not trying to change your opinion. I just object to those opinions being passed out in my classroom," she said. "The morale of these kids can be undermined if they start thinking the people, the grownups, are fools and incomp—"

"Starbuck and I were criticizing one guy," he told her. "Boxey heard us. You're not doing any of the children any good if you try to give them the idea that grownups are all perfect and it's only kids who screw up."

"What they learn ought to be decided by me and not—"

"Whoa now," said Apollo, putting his hand on her slim shoulder. "Everybody is running at a high pitch today. So let's call a truce, Athena. Okay?"

She turned away from him for a few seconds, studying the rivets in the wall. "Okay, but . . . well, don't make Boxey cynical before his time."

"I'm trying not to," said Apollo.

Athena faced him, taking a deep breath. "What do you really think'll happen?" she asked. "Will these people be able to tell us something?"

"I sure hope so," Apollo answered.

CHAPTER SIX

Lieutenant Boomer was slouched slightly in his chair, chin resting on his fist, and staring out of one of the lounge's view windows. He turned away from contemplating the vastness of space when Apollo joined him at his table. "You don't look much like the conquering hero," he observed.

"Don't feel much like one."

The black lieutenant frowned. "You and Starbuck brought home the bacon," he said. "You ought to be feeling proud, respected and so on."

Apollo shook his head. "Guess I'm having second thoughts. And I'm also worrying about what's going to happen to those six people."

"How so? We're doing all we can for them, aren't we?"

"It's risky, fooling with their life support system," Apollo said. "Maybe we just ought to let them alone.

31

Four of them are just children, you know, and the idea
of tinkering with kids makes me damn uneasy."

Boomer said, "I don't think we ought to leave them
alone. These folks are the first humans we've encountered who are from some other civilization for sure."

"We've encountered humans before."

"Nope, not since we left range of our own planet
systems," said Boomer, leaning toward his friend.
"Everybody we've bumped into up to now, Apollo, has
been a drifter or a pioneer from one of our own worlds.
Whatever colony or outpost we've come across, the pop-
ulation has been like that."

"Even so."

"But even if a few of the humans we've run across
were descendants of the lost thirteenth tribe, they were
just stragglers left behind," continued Boomer, his voice
intense. "Now, right here on this ship of ours, we have
human life forms that are from a technologically advanced civilization. But a civilization different from anything we've ever hit before. And that, to my way of
thinking, is what the whole point of this voyage of *Galactica* has been."

"The lad's right," said Starbuck, strolling up and taking the third chair at the table. "That is why we've risked
our lives and kept on residing in tin cans rather than
stopping at one of the planets we've passed that could've
supported life."

Apollo made his right hand into a fist and rested it
on the table top. "That's not exactly the way I heard it,
good buddy."

Starbuck grinned and signaled to an orderly to bring
him an ambrosia. "Tell me your version of the truth,
Uncle Apollo."

"We've kept moving across space because we're a
hunted people. We haven't really been strong enough to

stop and settle, because we aren't certain we can defend ourselves."

"Aw," said Starbuck, "we haven't seen a Cylon in sectons. I say we've just been dealt a terrific hand and we have to play it out. We're going to win, too."

"Starbuck, you're a nifty viper pilot and the best fighting man in the fleet," said Apollo, "but—"

"Stop there," suggested Starbuck as his drink arrived. "I like flattery, but not the criticism I have a hunch is coming."

"But you have a damn annoying habit of thinking in absolutes," Apollo went on. "We win, we lose. We find Earth, we don't. A girl says yes, she says no. The quality of civilization is determined by the values placed between extremes."

Starbuck took a slow sip of his drink. "Would you run that by once more, that last part? It sounds profound enough for me to copy it down and have it embroidered on a pillow or something. 'The quality of . . .' How'd the rest go?"

Shaking his head, Apollo said, "I know how Athena must feel, trying to drum some knowledge into a bunch of restless kids."

"Wait now," said Starbuck, grinning. "Athena I'd listen to. In fact just about any pretty lady has a heck of a good chance of reaching me with her message."

After a few seconds Boomer said, "You were about to make some other point, Apollo. Before the hotshot here came traipsing in."

"Traipsing? Are you insinuating that I—"

"I've just been thinking about those six wayfarers," said Apollo. "Especially the four children, but all of them really. I don't know, when we were out there and we saw that ship of theirs I was elated. Here it was, a chance to get more input about Earth. So we brought them here."

"Which," said Starbuck, "was absolutely the smart thing to do, old chum."

"Maybe."

"Maybe?"

"It's been occurring to me, especially when I see Salik and Wilker and a whole army of doctors and technicians swarming all over the craft, that the best thing to do would be to let them continue on their way unmolested."

"You mean like taking out the hook and tossing the fish back into the stream after landing it?" asked Boomer.

"These six aren't plunder," said Apollo. "They're people and we've interfered with them. We may very well keep them from ever fulfilling their mission."

Starbuck made an exasperated noise and popped a fresh cigar between his teeth. "Now, Boomer, you see what it's like working with this guy," he said. "He never turns that brain of his off, it's working around the clock. Going back over what we've done, trying to find a way to worry about some dinky trivial thing."

"You guys did the right thing," said Boomer. "I'd have done exactly the same thing if I'd spotted that ship while on scout patrol."

"That doesn't make it right," said Apollo.

"You really want to let these people go, old chum?" Starbuck studied his friend's face. "Push 'em out of the docking bay and let 'em get on with their trip?"

"It might be the best course, yes."

"But we don't know where they're bound for," said Starbuck, lighting his cigar with an angry flick of his lighter. "If we toss them out into space that crate may just turn into a derelict. I mean, it could be it long ago forgot where they were suppposed to be going."

"No, I think the ship is capable, if we don't tamper too much more with it, of delivering its passengers to the right destination."

"You're being dippy," said Starbuck. "You see a curly-headed little kid dozing in a glass coffin and you get mushy. These six people are important to us. We have to find out what it is they know."

"Sometimes the price you have to pay for knowledge is just too high," said Apollo.

At the next table a chubby young man in the uniform of a security guard leaned back and turned toward them. "If anyone's interested in my vote," he said in his nasal voice, "I'm with Starbuck. I say let's go in there and open those damn boxes quick. We have to start interrogating those people, because the lives of every damn one of us depend on what they know."

Starbuck scanned the plump youth. "You're Reese, aren't you?"

"Sure, you know—"

"Reese, you have ten seconds to withdraw your snoot from our conversation," said Starbuck, grinning thinly. "After which time I will personally carry you bodily to the nearest wastechute and eject you into the vastness of space."

"Listen, Starbuck, I was only—"

"Say no more," warned Starbuck, pushing back his chair and raising a cautionary hand.

"Geeze, a guy tries to help you out and you come on like—"

"The day I need a nitwit sec officer to fight my battles, that will be the day they—"

"Starbuck," said Apollo, putting a restraining hand on Starbuck's arm and keeping him from hopping up out of his chair, "do your fighting on the triad courts, okay?"

The security officer stood up. "I'm not the only one who feels like this," he told them. "We can't let those six get away and we have to do whatever's necessary to find out everything they know. If they're human, they breathe fresh air and so there's no need to worry about breaking them out of their boxes." He took a deep breath, face reddening. "Speaking of fresh air, I need some. Being around you, Starbuck, always gives me the bends." He went stomping off.

Boomer watched his departure. "And here I been hearing so much about your winning personality, Starbuck."

"I should've popped him one in the—"

"My friend," said Apollo, gradually letting go of his arm, "you are forgetting the main purpose of the lounge. It's a place to relax."

Starbuck settled down some in his chair. "Well, damn it, I get unsettled when a nitwit like that starts agreeing with me."

"You stay here and rethink the whole thing." Apollo rose up. "I'm going to see how the doctors are coming."

"I'll tag along," offered Starbuck.

"They don't need a crowd down there," said Apollo. "I'll fill you in soon as I know anything new."

Nodding, Starbuck picked up his glass. "I'm not voting to risk those kids' lives either, you know," he said.

"I know." Apollo left the table.

CHAPTER SEVEN

An unexpected sizzle of yellowish sparks came sputtering out of the wall and showered down on the glass coffin that held the sleeping young woman.

"Damn!" exclaimed Doctor Wilker.

"Watch out, take it easy," warned Doctor Salik anxiously. He was hunched at a row of dials and gauges.

Wilker withdrew the hand-held probing tool he'd been using to test the complex wiring system in the life support room. "I seem to have shorted out a line," he said puzzled. "Which is odd, since this whole setup looks simple and easy to—"

"There was a temporary drop on every indicator here. Power, gases, everything," said Salik to his colleague. "I'd say you struck a central nerve of the whole system."

"Well, at least we're getting closer."

"You might have shorted out their whole ship," said

Salik, angry. "You can't keep going this way or we'll kill them all."

"I'm being as careful and thorough as I can under the circumstances," said Wilker. "I really do believe, doctor, that we don't have time to move at the pace you'd prefer to—"

"We have all the time we need."

"Oh, do we? Already Councilman Geller has been trying to get in here to talk to these people," said Wilker. "I am not about to cross the Council of Twelve or jeopardize my—"

"It's these people's lives you ought to be worrying about," said Apollo as he stepped across the threshold.

"We don't need your interference just now, Captain," said Wilker. "I'd advise you to—"

"Have you learned anything?"

"We've found that the gas being used is stored in liquid form and is regenerated and recycled," said Wilker impatiently. "Now if you'll toddle off, we'll determine exactly how—"

"You don't seem to share your associate's optimism," Apollo said to Doctor Salik.

"I would prefer to work at a much slower rate, to make a good many more tests before we—"

"There's not time," cut in Wilker.

"I heard you mentioning Geller," said Apollo. "But he has no authority over this—"

"Oh, doesn't he? It isn't wise to cross the Council, Captain."

Turning his back on the scientist, Apollo addressed Salik. "Are things going wrong?"

"Well, as we probe the circuits in here, we occasionally short out lines, thereby draining off energy."

"It's nothing critical," insisted Wilker.

Salik shook his head. "There are still many things we

don't know," he told Apollo. "We don't yet know how far it is to Earth nor how far they've come. Therefore, we can't as yet determine how long this system will support their lives. I'd like—"

"I want you both to discontinue your work at once," said Apollo decisively.

Wilker blinked. "You don't, young man, have the authority to—"

"I say I do." He caught hold of the scientist's arm. "I want you out of this ship at once. Doctor Salik, you stay here and monitor the situation, but don't do anything more."

"Very well," said Salik, rubbing his hand along his side thoughtfully.

"You and I, Wilker, will go talk to my father," said Apollo.

"By all means," said Wilker with a chill smile. "I wouldn't miss seeing Commander Adama's face when you tell him what you've tried to do, Captain."

Commander Adama was frowning at the image on the communication screen. "I think I've already made myself perfectly clear," he said evenly. "You can tell the Council, Councilman Geller, that until I am absolutely persuaded that—"

"Then you're refusing me entry to this captured ship?"

"The vehicle was not captured. It was brought in to the docking bay simply to—"

"Whatever you want to call the blasted thing," cut in the impatient councilman, "we of the Council believe we have the right to make an inspection."

"Not at this time."

"When then do you—"

"You'll be informed, Geller," said Adama. He flicked off the screen.

Leaving his chair, the commander made a slow circuit of his quarters.

A speaker just over the doorway cut in on his thoughts by announcing, "Captain Apollo and Doctor Wilker to see you."

"Show them in."

The door hissed open and his son came striding in, followed by the sardonically smiling scientist.

"I'll let this hotheaded offspring of yours explain the rather nasty situation that's developed," Wilker said.

"Sit down," Adama invited, settling into a chair. "What's been going on, Apollo?"

"I ordered the scientific team to quit working on the ship," his son explained, ignoring the chair he'd nodded at.

"That doesn't seem to be in our best interests."

"They're running a risk of shutting off the whole support system," explained Apollo, pacing. "Doctor Salik apparently has the patience to do the job right, but Doctor Wilker is rushing things."

"Just because I don't crawl along like that—"

"He's caused some damage already," accused Apollo, pointing at the scientist. "There's a possibility that, if he's allowed to keep tinkering, he'll abort the whole business and kill every damned one of those people."

"I'd hardly characterize my work as tinkering, Captain." Carefully Wilker lowered himself to a stuffed chair.

Adama glanced at him. "Was there some danger?"

"Not at all."

"But you had some sort of accident?"

"Well, there were a few shorts," admitted Wilker. "And, yes, it did cause the power to diminish. Nothing terribly serious as far as I—"

"If that support system fails, they die," said Apollo. "That is sure as hell serious."

Adama stroked his chin. "You took a good deal on yourself, Apollo."

"I didn't think there was time for a vote."

"You showed a certain amount of guts, doing what you did," said his father, with a trace of approval in his voice. "However, I don't actually—"

"Commander," broke in Doctor Wilker, "I didn't get around to mentioning this to your impetuous cub here, but we found an operations manual in that craft. The ship is most definitely from Earth."

Apollo said, "That doesn't give you the right to risk their lives, Doctor."

The commander said, "I'd like to see that manual as soon as possible."

"It's built into the bridge instrumentation," answered Wilker. "The reference to Earth appeared on a monitor relating to the relative gravity in leaving Earth's atmosphere and that of a place called Lunar Seven."

"Lunar Seven," said Adama. "Then this is actually as important as we—"

"What you both seem to be avoiding is the fact," said Apollo, "that we've seized a foreign craft and interrupted its perfectly legitimate course between two unknown points."

"You can't categorize what we've done as an illegal seizure," his father said quietly.

"What else do you call it when you take a ship out of flight and then tamper with it until its power sources begin to fail?"

"There has been a slight power loss, granted," said Wilker. "But that's to be expected."

The commander studied his son for a few silent seconds. "I'm not sure I know what your point is, Apollo," he said finally.

"My point is we made a mistake," he said. "Starbuck

and me, you and these science boys and the Council. We're all wrong."

"That's not what you were saying earlier."

"I was buoyed by the discovery," answered Apollo, "acting like a kid. Now, after thinking, after seeing those people asleep and trusting in those glass coffins . . . well, we're wrong. Doctor Wilker and Doctor Salik shouldn't be allowed to go on."

Steepling his fingers over his broad chest, Commander Adama asked, "What alternate course of action do you think we have open to us?"

Apollo spread his hands wide. "Let them go."

"Let them go?"

"Right, put them back on their original course."

The commander left his chair. "In doing that, Apollo, we'd lose any chance of communicating with them."

"Even if they stay here, there's a good chance they'll die before we can talk to them anyway," his son said. "Four children and a man and woman."

"You're allowing, if I may intrude in a family squabble," said Doctor Wilker, "sentiment to outweigh logic. I tell you this craft is definitely from Earth and therefore what these six may have to impart to us is of considerable importance—"

"I doubt those little kids have anything to tell us," said Apollo.

"You know what I mean," said Wilker, dismissing the interruption with an annoyed wave of the hand. "We're in the business of taking risks, not of running a nursery for every stray—"

"Commander," said the speaker over the entrance, "Councilman Geller insists on seeing you. At once."

Adama nodded at his son. "Don't get into a fight with him," he cautioned. "Very well, let him in."

The door whispered open and the councilman entered.

His chins were fluttering and his Council robes flapped out behind him as he hurried in. "Since you hung up on me, Commander, I had no other choice but to come here in person."

"I had assumed our conversation was at an end," said Adama.

"On the contrary, it had hardly begun," said Geller, every pound of him looking unhappy. "We have people, important people, arriving on the *Galactica*. All of them, each and every one of them, interested in the same thing— the secrets to be wrested from the voyagers who repose at this very minute in the—"

"This sounds like a campaign speech," said Apollo under his breath.

"...Therefore, Commander, I have been sent by the Council itself, the awesome body which is responsible for the efficient running of the vast—"

"What exactly do you want?" asked Adama.

"We want to know why you've been so inactive," he said. "While we're reluctant to take matters out of your competent hands, we can't sit around idle while you do nothing. I won't even bother to protest the rude treatment I and several other very important officials have suffered by not being allowed so much as a glimpse at the most significant find we've ever made. No, suffice it to say that the Council would like to take the burden of being solely responsible for this situation off your capable shoulders, Commander Adama."

"Just how will you do that, Councilman Geller?"

"Why don't we simply take a vote of the Council?"

His brows furrowed, Adama turned to his son. "Apollo, I'm putting you in charge of the security of that ship," he said. "Very well, Geller, call the Council into session at once."

CHAPTER EIGHT

Doctor Salik ducked his head slightly as he stepped out of the mystery ship. He wiped the back of his hand across his forehead. "Going to be some time yet," he said.

Starbuck had been crouching near the craft. Taking his cigar out of his mouth, he stood and said, "You may not have as much time as you thought, Doc."

Salik noticed the growing cluster of people on the other side of the see-through restraining wall. "I'd like it if all these gawkers were herded elsewhere."

"Some of them are Council members," said Apollo. "And the security force is reluctant to prod them."

"Anything new inside?" Starbuck asked the doctor.

"Nothing encouraging," he said. "I'm going up to talk to the commander. You'll see to it that no one gets inside."

"That we will," promised Starbuck.

"That no one includes you fellows." Salik walked up

to the doorway in the wall and signaled to a security guard.

A husky young man activated the door release and the door hissed open. "You don't have to worry about anyone getting in there, Doctor Salik," he said. "We'll contain the crowd until the orders arrive."

"What orders?"

"Well, the Council is voting right now to terminate the life support systems and let those folks in there out of their coffins."

"You can't let them do that." He shook his head angrily. "Apollo, Starbuck, see to it that that doesn't happen."

"Not to worry, Doc. Nobody'll get by us," Starbuck assured him. "You go on up and tell the commander what's going on."

Nodding absently, the doctor pushed his way through the crowd in the corridor.

Before closing the door, the guard said, "You seem to have a goofy idea of the way things work, Starbuck."

Starbuck rubbed his right fist. "I know how this works, pal," he said.

"The point being, we're in charge here," the security guard informed him. "I'd hate to have to tangle with you over—"

"This is a military bay," said Apollo. "You and your men only have jurisdiction over civilians aboard the *Galactica.*"

The guard shrugged. "We'll see." He shut the door.

"Halfwit," commented Starbuck, rubbing at his fist again. "Seems to me the Council ought to be voting on how to get smarter guys into security ranks."

"Save your anger," advised Apollo. "We're probably going to have to hold off more important gents than him."

The dark-haired young man was the first to awaken.
A new humming started up in the walls and then the
lights began to glow brighter. A row of lights mounted
over the head of his glass coffin ceased burning pale
green and started burning an intense red. The scarlet glow
bathed the sleeping man.

His eyes, slowly, opened.

Gradually awareness came back into his face. He began flexing the fingers of his right hand. After a moment
the young man reached up and pressed his forefinger
against a silver button on the wall of the case which held
him.

A new humming commenced. Very gradually the lid
of the glass box swung open.

The young man, taking in a careful breath, sat up and
looked around. "We must've arrived," he muttered in a
dry, weak voice.

He took another breath and then climbed out of the
coffin. His legs shook and wobbled as he tried to stand
up. He put out a hand, steadied himself against the metal
wall. He ran his tongue over his lips several times and
shook his head slowly from side to side.

"Atmosphere in here," he said to himself, "doesn't
seem quite right."

Swaying some, he made his way to a small view
window and looked out. He frowned, mouth opening,
and then pulled his head back.

He shook his head and began to inspect the other glass
boxes. He looked in on the children first. "All okay,"
he said after a few moments.

From a slash pocket in his one-piece grey jumpsuit
he took a small plastic card.

Kneeling at the foot of the coffin that held the blonde young woman, he slid the rectangle of yellow into a thin slot at its base. "I think I better talk to Sarah," he said, breathing shallowly.

A thin humming seemed to come from beneath the girl's coffin. Then the lid rose up.

"Sarah? Are you okay?" the young man asked, leaning toward the girl.

Her eyelids fluttered. She opened her eyes and looked up at him with no sign of recognition.

"Sarah, it's me. Michael."

A faint smile came to her lips. "Michael? Is the journey over? What's the—"

"Something's gone wrong," he said, taking her hand carefully.

Sarah glanced around. "Are the children—"

"They're fine," Michael answered. "I haven't revived them yet, because . . . well, because I frankly don't know where we are."

"I don't understand," she said. "You're awake and you awakened me. If we haven't arrived at Lunar Seven then why were you reactivated?"

"Sarah, I'm not certain," he told the young woman. "We seem to be inside a larger space craft. It's like nothing I've ever seen, so—"

"Then you don't think we've been captured by—"

"Not by them, no," he replied.

"Who then?"

"They're humans, the ones I got a glimpse of when I looked out the window."

"Then are they the ones who revived you?"

He shook his dark head. "Our ship may have assumed we'd ended the journey," he said. "My being awakened might just be the result of a malfunction of some kind. I just don't know."

She started to get out of the glass coffin. "We'll have to find out," she said. "No matter who has diverted us, we have to confront them and tell them right out that they can't do—"

"Easy now, Sarah," he said, smiling at her. "Get control of your temper."

"It's not a temper," she said. "I simply don't let anyone push me around. These people who've captured us, no matter who they may be or who they think they are, have no right whatsoever to do this. We'll just march right out and tell them what—"

"No, no," he said, putting a restraining hand on her shoulder. "Not just yet, Sarah. I want you to stay here with the kids."

"While you're doing what?"

"I want to scout around a bit," he said. "Find out what I can."

"There's no reason I can't do that," Sarah said. "I'm as good as you are at—"

"I know, I know," he said. "But you're better with the children than I am. Please, now, Sarah, stay here. I'll be back soon."

After a few seconds she took his hand in hers. "Watch your temper, too," she said. "Don't let them hurt you."

"I won't," he promised.

It was chill in the large domed meeting chamber of the Council and in the brief silences between verbal exchanges the faint metallic chattering of the air circulation systems could be heard.

Councilman Geller, a look of satisfaction on his plump face, was saying, "Very well. It has been decided. Since the support systems are failing anyway, we will, therefore, remove these humans from their ship as quickly and expediently as possible."

Commander Adama said, "We can't do that. You just heard Doctor Salik tell you it might well kill them."

"We'll be as careful and prudent as possible," Geller assured him, rubbing at one of his chins. "We'll begin with the oldest member among our space voyagers. He would undoubtedly be the one most likely to—"

"Gentlemen, you still don't understand," said Salik, rising up out of his chair.

"We understand very well, and have voted accordingly," Geller reminded him.

Doctor Salik shook his head from side to side once. "I will not be responsible for any of—"

"But you're not responsible, we are," said the fat councilman. "The responsibility is ours, you are merely carrying out the will of the Council."

"No, I can't."

"Doctor, let me remind you that you have been ordered to do this."

Salik took a step back from the vast table. "Let me remind you, Councilman, that you'll have to find another doctor." He pivoted on his heel and went walking out of the room.

When the startled murmuring faded, Geller turned to Adama. "Commander, go talk to him."

Slowly the commander rose up. "Oh, I intend to, yes," he said.

"Excellent. Explain his duties to him and—"

"Actually, I plan to tell him that I'm quite proud of him," said Adama, smiling to himself. "Somehow, lately, I've been seeing fewer and fewer men standing up for the things they believe in."

"You can't go condoning insubordination," said Geller, puffing. "The morale of the—"

"I suggest you gentlemen reconsider your vote," said the commander as he walked toward an exitway. "I'd hate to see this lead to a battle between us."

"Ah, but it won't come to that," said Geller, with a bit less than complete conviction.

"Don't bet on it, sir," said Adama.

CHAPTER NINE

Starbuck and Apollo stood with their backs to the open entryway of the ship.

"That smirk on Wilker's face doesn't cheer me," said Starbuck, chomping down on his cigar.

The scientist, flanked by two security guards, was hurrying up to the Earth ship.

"It's my sad duty," said Doctor Wilker, smiling smugly, "to inform you that you've lost. The Council has voted and the six passengers are to be revived at once."

"You've got to be kidding," said Starbuck. "The whole damn Council can't be as dimwitted as you."

One of the security men said, "Better step aside."

"I assure you the vote is official," said Wilker. Turning, he gestured toward the wall of plastic. "Since I can't get any co-operation from the people aboard the *Galactica*, I've summoned two very efficient, and obedient, Med Techs from another ship of the fleet."

Lowering his head, Starbuck rubbed his hands together. "What say, Apollo?" he inquired. "Think we can persuade these gents to keep out?"

Apollo gave a negative shake of his head. "It's no use," he said. "We can't go against the Council."

"Oh, no?" Starbuck said. "I've done it before and, chum, I'm more than ready to—"

"Good lord!" Wilker was looking beyond Starbuck, his face suddenly pale.

Starbuck's eyebrows climbed. "Really scared you this time, huh?"

Nudging him, Apollo said quietly, "Behind you."

Starbuck turned to see a tall slender young man standing just inside the doorway of the ship, a strange-looking silver pistol in his right hand. "Don't come any closer, any of you," he said. His voice was slightly blurred and unsteady.

Starbuck laughed. "Hey, they woke up on their own. That's terrific."

"One of them did, anyway," said Apollo. He took a step toward the dark-haired young man, holding out his hand. "Welcome to the *Galactica*. I'm Captain Apollo and—"

"Please, stay where you are."

"Listen," said Starbuck, "we aren't going to hurt you, buddy. In fact, we've been risking our butts to see that nobody did you any harm."

Doctor Wilker was scanning the young man. "We mean you no harm," he said in a different tone of voice than the one he'd been using. "I am a scientist and I want merely to come aboard and help you. You and the others."

One of the security guards said, "No use babying these people." He pushed by the doctor and started for the entrance. "We're coming in now."

The gun in the dark young man's hand hummed. A beam of yellow light came knifing out of its barrel to hit the charging guard's broad chest.

The guard made a sudden surprised whimpering sound. His hands started up to clutch his chest, but then his fingers went slack. He collapsed to the floor like a sack of dirty laundry.

"Impressive," said Starbuck, glancing from the fallen man to the gun.

Wilker dropped to the guard's side and took hold of his wrist. "He's alive," he said. "That thing is some kind of stunner."

"It can kill, too," said the young man. "If I want it to." He took one step out of the ship. "I would prefer not to kill any of you."

"So would we," said Starbuck. "Live and let live, that's our motto."

Apollo said, "I can see why you're uneasy. We ought to just talk and see if we can't come to some sort of—"

"I want to know why we've been brought here," the young man said. He was taking rapid, short breaths and his face was getting paler as he stood there.

"Well, we didn't mean any harm," began Apollo, taking a step nearer. "See, you and I . . . all of us really are brothers."

"No, that's not true." He gestured at the docking bay and the people in it. "None of this is familiar to me. There's not a one of you dressed in any style I know."

"Brothers," said Apollo, "who were separated, we think, quite awhile ago. We've been searching for—"

"What is this place? It doesn't seem to be an abandoned Lunar post."

"You're aboard a ship," said Apollo. "We call it a battlestar and it's named *Galactica*. We're part of—"

The young man looked straight up. "The size of the thing..." His left hand fluttered and he reached out to try to catch hold of something.

Instead he dropped to his knees. He gasped, shivered and then toppled forward. His face smacked into the floor and he lay still.

"Hellsfire!" exclaimed Starbuck. "Is the guy dead?"

"Don't touch him!"

It was Doctor Salik, who had just arrived on the scene. Cassiopea was with him.

"I'm perfectly capable of handling this," Wilker assured his colleague.

Ignoring him, Salik crouched beside the young man. "He's having a severe respiratory problem."

"It's the atmospheric density," said Cassiopea.

"Yes, that's it," agreed Doctor Salik. "Apollo, you and Starbuck rush this man to a decomp chamber. Cassie, he'll need about one fifth of our own atmosphere to thrive, I think."

"Hadn't you better come along?" asked Apollo as he and the lieutenant carefully picked up the young man.

"After I see to those inside," the doctor said. "With luck we may be able to save them all. No thanks to you," he told Wilker as he climbed into the ship.

Pressing a palm against his chest, Doctor Wilker said, "I had nothing to do with this. Nothing at all."

The blonde young woman had fallen to one knee. Her face was pale and tinged with blue. "What...what have you...done with...Michael?"

"He's being taken care of. There's nothing to worry about," Doctor Salik assured her as he moved closer. "I'm here only to help you, so you don't need that weapon, young woman."

There was a silver pistol dangling from her weak fingers. "Who . . . who are you?"

"My name is Salik, I'm a doctor. A medical doctor." He moved to her side and knelt.

"I . . . my name is . . . Sarah," she said, gasping in air. "I don't . . . understand why . . . I'm having such trouble . . . breathing. . . ."

"You're simply not used to the same sort of atmosphere that we are, Sarah." He slid a reassuring arm around her slim shoulders. "Come along with me and I'll see to it that—"

"The children . . ." As she spoke the gun dropped from her slack fingers, bouncing once on the lid of one of the glass boxes. "You . . . mustn't hurt them. . . ."

"Will they be revived automatically, the way you and Michael were?"

Sarah shook her head. "Only Michael," she answered. "He was to awaken when we reached Lunar Seven . . . then revive me and we . . . we'd revive the four children. But this . . . this isn't where we're supposed to be. . . ."

"No, it isn't," Salik said, helping her to her feet.

CHAPTER TEN

In the center of a vast whiteness sat two grey respirator units. They, too, looked somewhat like coffins and held Michael and Sarah.

Doctor Salik was leaning over the one that was aiding the blonde young woman. "They both seem to be doing fine," he said.

Starbuck took a thoughtful chew on his dead cigar. "Fine? They're flat on their backs and out cold."

"I should, falling back on an old medical cliche, have said they were doing as well as could be expected," said the doctor, making a delicate adjustment on one of the dials of Sarah's breathing tank.

Apollo said, "Meaning exactly what, Doctor?"

Putting his hands in his pockets and gazing up at the rimmed ceiling of this wing of the Medical Center, Salik said, "As long as they stay in these respirators they'll be fine."

"That doesn't make for a very fun-filled life style," said Starbuck.

"No, but it's better than being dead," answered the physician.

"Slightly," said Starbuck. "I'm starting to think we never should've—"

"Let me outline the problem to you once more," offered Salik, facing the impatient lieutenant. "It's the pressure of our environment here on the *Galactica*. It was literally starting to crush them. Our air pressure is substantially stronger than what they are accustomed to."

"But they're human, like us, so they ought to have been in an environment very much like this," said Captain Apollo.

"We're adaptable," said Doctor Salik. "It may be that over many millennia their environment, the air they breathe, grew thinner. Very gradually so that the majority of them could adapt to it easily."

"Or our environment may have grown heavier," said Apollo.

Salik nodded and shrugged. "It really doesn't matter," he said. "The important thing is they're not able to function in our world here."

"And they can never come out of these tanks?" asked Starbuck.

"You saw what happened to Michael," said Salik.

Starbuck eyed Apollo. "We are, old chum, going to have to do something about this," he said firmly.

Commander Adama stood at the view window in his quarters. His forehead was furrowed. "We came very close to finding other humans," he said. "Perhaps the very tribe from Earth we seek."

Clearing his throat, Colonel Tigh said, "There's no good reason why we can't sustain them, in hopes that they'll regain enough strength to communicate with us."

Apollo and Starbuck were sitting, uneasy, in twin chairs across the room. Apollo said, "We can't do that."

Tigh scowled. "We are in need of answers, Captain," he said. "Indeed, the lives of every man, woman and child in this fleet may well depend on the answers. We have to know if Earth can support us, if she is technically advanced enough to help us ward off our enemies. Can Earth protect herself if a Cylon invasion were to—"

"I know what you're saying," cut in Apollo. "The thing is, Colonel, these six lives don't belong to us. No matter how important we may think these people may be to our own future."

"Surely, Captain, as a military man," said the colonel, "you must understand that in some situations the lives of the few must be risked for the good of the many. That's sound thinking in—"

"We can't do that this time," insisted Apollo.

Adama watched his son for a few silent seconds. "You and Starbuck are the ones who brought these wayfarers to us, Apollo," he reminded.

"That was a mistake, as I've said before," Apollo told him. "We shouldn't have done it."

"This is absolutely ridiculous," said Tigh. "Sitting around like a bunch of guilty children and bewailing the—"

"Wait now," said the commander. "Apollo, what are you getting at?"

"It's simple," his son answered. "We had no right to interrupt their journey. We have to let them continue on their way."

Adama crossed to a large armchair and seated himself. "Suppose their support systems are no longer capable of carrying them safely to their destination?"

"The support systems can be put back in first class

order," said Apollo. "That's not a problem."

"Suppose," suggested Colonel Tigh, "we turn them loose and they run smack into a Cylon attack?"

"Hell, we haven't seen a Cylon in sectons," said Starbuck, shifting in his seat.

"And I'll take a team of volunteers with their ship to protect it on its voyage," said Apollo.

Steepling his fingers, Adama rested his strong chin on them. "You've been doing quite a bit of thinking about this."

"I have, yes," said Apollo. "Some of what I think . . . no, make that what I feel." He nodded at the colonel. "This isn't based on logic entirely, nor on sound military thinking and planning." He leaned back in his chair, took a slow deep breath. "I feel that this family, these six people, are being beckoned to some specific destination. And there, maybe, we can also find some of the answers that we need."

The commander lowered his hands, rested his palms on his knees. "Our life systems seem incompatible."

"No, it's not exactly that," said Apollo. "I've kicked some of these notions around with Doctor Salik and he agrees. You see, these people, our reluctant guests, can't accept the weight of our pressurization. But we, on the other hand, have all experienced short terms in environments with far less pressure than our own. Where they're going, I believe we can survive."

"And if you're wrong?" asked Colonel Tigh.

"That's a risk we'll have to take," answered Apollo. "Weren't you just talking about the few taking a chance for the many?"

"Being pigheaded and foolish wasn't exactly what I—"

"If anybody's pigheaded hereabouts," put in Lieutenant Starbuck, "meaning no offense, sir, it isn't the captain here."

"Oh, really?" Tigh glowered at Starbuck. "See here, Starbuck, your cocky attitude may charm certain—"

"Gentlemen," said Adama quietly. "I'd like to think we're above squabbling at important times like this." He crossed to a communications screen in the wall and punched out a number.

The screen popped to life and then Doctor Salik appeared. "Yes, Commander?" He glanced back over his shoulder, as though anxious to get back to what he'd been doing.

"Doctor, I have the impression you and my son have been conspiring," Adama said.

Salik shrugged. "I simply expressed my opinions to Apollo," he replied. "Opinions backed up, I might add, with one hell of a lot of facts."

"Then let me make sure I understand you. The only chance these people have of surviving is to be allowed to continue on with their journey?"

"They can survive here on *Galactica* if we keep them permanently imprisoned in depressurized cannisters."

"With no guarantee we'd ever be able to communicate with them?"

"That's right," answered the doctor. "I can't rule out the possibility that eventually we might be able to work out some means of—"

"I see, thank you." Adama killed the image on the screen.

"Well?" said his son, watching him return to his chair.

"You realize the Council would have to approve of letting the ship go."

"There isn't time for a political debate," said Starbuck. "Those bureaucrats'll kick this around for eons and still not get to an answer. Meantime—"

"Suppose we suggest that this is a military problem, pure and simple," said Apollo, sitting up and grinning.

"I don't quite see—"

"One of our visitors gunned down a security guard, didn't he?"

"Right," said Starbuck. "Therefore we'd be justified in taking decisive action to remove further threats of—"

"The guard was only stunned," said Colonel Tigh.

"The wisest course," said Apollo, "would be for Starbuck and me...that is if you volunteer for this, good buddy?"

Giving him a mock salute, Starbuck answered, "Include me in."

"For Starbuck and me to remove the possibility of any further danger to the fleet," continued Apollo. "That we do by placing the hostile craft back on its original course."

"The Council will never sit still for that," said Tigh.

"But we'll be able to assure the Council that the Earth ship is still under our control," said Apollo. "Because we'll be escorting it to its destination."

"Basically," said the colonel, "you're trying to flim-flam the Council and—"

The communication screen buzzed.

Adama activated it and found Councilman Geller's chubby face glaring at him from the screen.

"The Council is considerably upset," began Geller. "The fleet is deeply concerned."

"Why is that?" asked the commander.

"We hear news that these space wayfarers of yours have come back to life and attempted to kill several security guards."

"The news has reached you in somewhat exaggerated form," Adama said to him.

"Be that as it may, you can't deny that there was shooting?"

"I cannot, no," said Adama. "In fact, Councilman, I can tell you that even now we are dealing with this situation."

Geller's chins waggled. "I should think so," he said. "Up to now, you know, we haven't been very pleased with the way you've handled things. We expect a full report as soon as possible." The screen went blank.

Chuckling, Adama said, "Usually I hang up on him."

"They want answers as soon as possible," said Apollo, rising and moving to his father's side. "My plan won't work unless we get moving right now, before the Council takes any further action."

The commander moved again to the view window. "I can't say yes," he said slowly, "and I can't say no."

"Good," said Colonel Tigh, bouncing once in his chair. "Then the mission is scrubbed."

"I didn't say that either," Adama said. "Am I making myself clear?"

Apollo nodded and caught Starbuck's arm. "Couldn't be clearer," he said. "Let's move."

"Righto." Starbuck popped up and followed the captain out of the room.

CHAPTER ELEVEN

Lieutenant Jolly was fidgeting, moving his ambrosia glass from side to side, tapping one booted foot on the lounge floor, tugging at one end of his moustache and then the other.

"A frenkel for your thoughts," said Zixi, smiling tentatively across the table at him.

"Hum?"

"Your mind," she observed, "seems to be wandering."

Hunching his broad shoulders, the plump lieutenant admitted, "I suppose it is. Excuse me, since I don't want to give you the idea—"

"Oh, that's perfectly okay. I'm used to people not paying attention to me."

"I am paying attention to you, Zixi," he insisted. "The thing is, I'm also thinking about this Earth ship Starbuck and Apollo went and fished out of space."

"I understand," the auburn-haired young woman said.

"As to why I'm used to being ignored, I have three older sisters and when I was growing up people were always fawning over them and ignor—"

"That's ridiculous. You're a darn pretty girl."

"Pretty, yes." She nodded in agreement. "But not stunning and gorgeous. My other three sisters are, each and every one of them. You take the eldest, Xaviera, for instance. Why, she—"

"Your folks like X, huh?"

"Quite a bit, yes," agreed the girl. "But let's not talk about my beautiful sisters. Tell me what's worrying you, Jolly."

He frowned. "Well, I got me the notion that these six space voyagers are damn important," he told her. "Important to all of us. They can tell us how to get to Earth or a reasonable facsimile thereof. Meaning we can maybe settle down for a spell and quit thinking about the Cylons and warfare and all."

"You'd like that?"

"Be a nice change, to walk on real earth again," he said, grinning in anticipation. "And get a sunburn and have a house to live in, with a front porch." He leaned forward, putting both big fists on the table top. "But what I'm worried about is the damn Council. I hear tell they just voted to wake up all the folks in that ship, grownups and kids alike. Right quick."

"That could be dangerous."

"Hell, it could kill 'em all," said Jolly glumly. "Before we even get a chance to find out a single fact about—"

"Jolly, pardon me for barging in on this romantic interlude of yours." Boomer had come striding up to tap him on the shoulder.

Blinking, Jolly inquired, "What's happening?"

Leaning down, Boomer lowered his voice. "Star-buck'd like us to lend a hand on a . . . um . . . special project. Can you come along right now?"

"Well, sure." He glanced at the girl. "You won't mind if I desert you for a bit?"

"Oh, no," Zixi said. "I'm used to it."

Hands behind his back, Doctor Salik stared down into the tank that held the sleeping Sarah. "I wonder . . ." he muttered to himself.

"How long they'll survive in this sort of a setup?" finished Apollo, who'd come into the medlab a moment earlier.

Salik glanced up. "Oh, yes, that, too," he said. "But also I've been brooding about what we're keeping them from, what important mission is unfulfilled."

"The Council's voted," reminded Cassiopea. "There's really nothing we can—"

"Don't be too sure," put in Apollo.

The young woman studied his face. "You're looking very smug," she observed. "Yes, you're wearing the sort of look one expects to see plastered on Starbuck's face. When he's plotting one of his audacious—"

"Cassie, Cassie, whatever will people say?" Starbuck had entered the white room. "If you keep talking about me continually, folks will say we're in—"

"What I'm always saying about you, Starbuck," she said, "everybody aboard the *Galactica* already knows. That you're a self-centered, conceited, pushy, over—"

"Enough, enough." He clapped his hands over his ears. "All this flattery will make me vain, kiddo."

"You're impossible."

"That, too." Shifting his cigar to a new position in his mouth, he stepped up close to Apollo. "Everything's set, old chum."

"What's set?" Salik wanted to know.

"Hasn't the captain explained?"

"I was leading up to it subtly," said Apollo, "until you came stomping in, good buddy."

"Nell's bells, we got no time for subtle." Starbuck planted his hands on his hips. "We're taking your patients."

The young woman took a step in his direction. "Taking them? What are you talking about, Starbuck? Taking them where?"

"Where they belong, Cassie," he answered. "Back to their ship."

"They can't survive in that—"

"Sure, they can," he said. "If it's back in space and doing what it's supposed to be doing. The whole crate is built to take care of this gang until they reach their destination."

Brow furrowed, she turned to the doctor. "Doctor Salik, you've got to stop them."

He sighed. "Cassie, I think I'm on their side," he said. "In fact, I think I'd better go along with them. To monitor the equipment and make certain all goes—"

"Along with them?" She looked from the doctor to the other two. "You mean you're going along? Leaving the *Galactica* and going—"

"We'll escort their ship," explained Apollo, "using our vipers. Seems the least we can do, since we fouled up their flight in the first place."

"On top of which, we'll find out what sort of a spot they're heading for," added Starbuck. "Might just be a spot we, too, can settle on. Can't you see it, Cassie, you and me strolling hand in hand over lush green sward. Leafy tree bows sheltering us as birds sing sweet lyrics over our—"

"The Council'll lop your foolish heads off," she said.

"Naw, they'd have to catch us to do anything to us," said Starbuck with a grin. "And we'll be long gone before they even get wind of this little caper, kiddo."

Apollo said, "We appreciate your offer of help, Doctor Salik, but you're too important to the fleet. You can't just leave."

"But someone ought to be aboard that craft, to make sure nothing goes wrong once it's back on its original flight pattern," the doctor insisted.

Starbuck removed his cigar from his mouth and studied its smoldering tip. "Cassie? What say you step forward?" he suggested. "Here's a chance to do a great service for humanity. On top of which, you get to go on a cruise with two of the most personable lads in the entire crew."

"You mean you're asking me to mutiny along with you?"

Apollo put a hand on her shoulder. "Hey, this isn't mutiny," he said. "We've already got a way figured to flimflam the Council into thinking this is an essential move. If it works, that is."

"Even so," she said.

"Cassie," said the doctor, "I think what they're going to do is the right thing. And just about the only chance we have to save these people."

She lowered her head and shut her eyes for nearly a full minute. Opening them again, she said, "Okay, count me in. But I still think it's mutiny."

The two portable decompression chambers were shrouded with white plyocloths. Starbuck and Apollo were hefting the first one, and Jolly and Boomer lugged the second. Cassie, looking none too happy, brought up the rear of the procession.

When they halted at the entryway to the captive ship, the young woman moved to the front of the line. "It's okay," she told the pair of security guards. "These empty decomp tubes are to be taken aboard this ship at once."

"Nobody's notified us about any—"

"If you'd like to check with Doctor Salik," she said, showing impatience, "please do."

The other guard eyed her and the four men. "What's the idea? I mean, why do you need—"

"The four remaining passengers are to be removed at once," she said firmly. "Surely you're aware that the Council has voted to remove them and attempt to revive them?"

"Sure, we know that," said the other guard, "but—"

"Time's awasting," remarked Starbuck.

The guard frowned in his direction. "How come you guys are so eager to help out now? Awhile ago, I hear, you were ready to clobber anybody who touched a hair of these brats' heads."

"We had a long talk with Doctor Salik," explained Apollo. "He, being a wise fellow, pointed out the error of our thinking to us."

"Indeed he did," seconded Starbuck. "And so you see us before you chomping at the bit . . . or is that champing? Anyhow, we're eager to help out. Because we now believe that what's good for the Council is good for us all."

Both guards laughed. One of them said, "Looks like you lost out in what you were trying to do, Apollo," he said.

"As long as these folks remain alive, I didn't lose," he replied. "Right now, though, we have to start transferring these kids out of their support systems and into these portable chambers as soon as possible."

The guard looked at him for a few seconds. "You sure changed sides fast."

"He's like that," said Starbuck, shifting his cigar to the other side of his mouth. "What say you move aside, chum? You're standing in the way of progress."

"Okay, go on aboard," said the guard.

"We really appreciate your cooperation," Starbuck told him sincerely.

CHAPTER TWELVE

It was while they were transferring Michael to his own suspension chamber that the young man began to come awake again.

Sarah had already been safely returned to hers and Cassie was able to announce, "I've got their suspension units functioning just fine."

"Good enough," said the relieved Apollo. "Now we can lug these decomp chambers off the ship and con the guards into thinking we're hauling away the first of the kids."

"Then all that needs to be done," added Starbuck, "is get this ship launched out into space again and back on its original course."

"That's all automatic, once we start her up," said Apollo.

"Sure, but...hey!" Starbuck noticed Michael first. "Our guest is awake."

Michael sat up in his glass coffin. "What . . . what the hell . . . are you doing . . . to us?"

"Trying to help you, chum," Starbuck assured him.

"I can't . . . can't see how you can say that," said the dark young man. "Don't you . . . don't you realize what you've done . . . by bringing us here . . . and fouling everything up?"

"Look, we're trying to undo the mess we made," said Apollo, crouching to face him. "We want to put you back on your original course. If we launch this craft, is it certain to resume—"

"Sarah," he said. "What have you done with her and the children?"

"The kids never left this room," said Cassie. "And Sarah has just been returned to the unit next to yours."

He leaned, saw the girl asleep next to him. He smiled faintly as he pressed his fingertips to the lid. "You haven't . . . yet . . . haven't yet explained to me . . . who you are," he said. "Are you . . . from the Eastern Alliance?"

Apollo shrugged. "Never heard of it," he admitted. "Suppose you—"

"But . . . how can you not know about the Eastern Alliance? Who are you and . . . what is all this?"

Apollo said, "It may take more time to explain than we have right now, Michael. But let me ask you something, are you from a planet known as Terra?"

Michael answered, "My people are . . . but I . . . Sarah and I . . . the children . . . we were all born on Lunar Seven. That's where we're escaping from. . . . But you must know that, since you waylaid us and—"

"Whoa," said Starbuck. "You mean you're going to Lunar Seven, don't you? That's what the manual we found here in this crate indicates."

Giving an impatient shake of his head, the young man said, "What you pried into was the standard manual that's in all these ships. But the preset course was away from Lunar Seven."

Apollo said, "We didn't stop you because we wanted to stop you from getting where you want to go, Michael. We just didn't know any better. See, we have some problems of our own and we were hoping you could help us solve 'em."

"I've really no reason to trust you," he said.

Cassie said, "We're not playing games with you and the others. We do want to help you. My name is Cassiopea and this is Captain Apollo and Lieutenant Starbuck. We all—"

"What's that foul thing that's smoldering in your mouth?" he asked Starbuck.

Puzzled, Starbuck took out his cigar and scrutinized it. "This? It's a cigar. A stogie. A cheroot," he said. "I smoke 'em."

"Why?"

"Well, it's...um...a habit I guess."

Apollo said, "Where were you bound for when we intercepted you?"

"I won't tell you that unless—"

"We want to help you get back on course," repeated Apollo. "Damn it, that's the truth."

"My ship knows its course," he said. "If you, as you claim, return us to space, then it will take us where we must go. It's been programmed to do that."

Apollo nodded slowly. "We'll help you," he said. "And we'd like some help from you, too."

"Who are you? You still haven't answered me."

"We're from another world," said Starbuck, returning his cigar to his mouth. "Refugees in a way."

"We come from a broken world," added Apollo. "We're searching for a way to protect our people."

"What does that have to do with me?"

"We believe we could settle on Earth," said Apollo. "Or possibly on this Lunar Seven you—"

"No, you couldn't." He gave several negative shakes of his head. "You must never go to Lunar Seven. Anyway, the Destroyers would completely destroy you before you got anywhere near there. We barely were able to—"

"Folks, I'm as interested in all this chitchat as the next fellow, but we got to move," said Starbuck. "Otherwise, all our backsides will end up in slings."

"You're right," acknowledged Apollo. "Michael, we have to get your ship free of the *Galactica* right away." He glanced at Cassie and then back at the young man. "Are you well enough to fly your ship clear of the docking bay?"

"Yes, I can do that."

Cassie said, "It's risky, Apollo. He might, before we can get the pressure in this ship back to what it was, have some kind of—"

"I know it's risky," said Apollo, moving toward the exit. "But it's the only way we can get this ship out of here. You're going to be here with him, Cassie. So that—"

"Okay," she said. "We'll do it. You get out of here and do what you have to do."

"If," said Michael, perplexed, "you're not with the Alliance, then who—"

"We're fellow humans," said Starbuck. "And humans have got to stick together against all the other critters one encounters whilst roving—"

"I don't quite get you," said Michael. "What do you mean about humans? Are there other kinds of life out there?"

"To put it succinctly," said Starbuck, "yep."

Apollo caught his arm. "We don't have time for your

usual discourse on the flora and fauna of space, Starbuck. Let's move."

"Righto. Cassie can explain some of the finer points to you," he said. "Now let's get Jolly and Boomer in here to help with the heavy lifting."

In the corridor leading to the landing bay Starbuck said, "Whoa, gang." He lowered his end of the decomp tank to the floor.

Apollo let down his end and stepped clear. "Okay, fellows, here's where the second part of your job comes in."

Jolly and Boomer set the unit they'd been hauling down on the pebbled metal floor.

"You guys are heading for one hell of a lot of trouble," observed Lieutenant Jolly, rubbing his big hands together. "So why not let us tag along to—"

"Nope," said Starbuck with a shake of his head. "Thanks for the offer, but two vipers are plenty for this job."

Boomer said, "Going to be a lot of fun here on the *Galactica* once everybody realizes what's going on."

"By that time," said Starbuck, relighting his cigar, "we'll be long gone."

"And now," suggested Apollo, "you two go in and do your bit toward distracting the security guards. So Cassie and our reluctant guest, Michael, can get that ship launched."

"Hell's going to break loose when that thing goes roaring out of here," said Jolly, chuckling.

"Which is why you've got to lure those guards out here," said Apollo. "They think we've got two of the kids in these gadgets, so when you rush in there and tell 'em there's been an accident out here to one of the units and you need their help, they'll come running."

"Everybody worries about a kid in trouble," added Starbuck. "Even a hardhearted sec guard."

"Once we get 'em out here and away from that ship, we do our darndest to keep 'em here," said Boomer, nodding at the doorway. "Have trouble with the door and such."

"That'll be a snap," said Jolly. "I worked a similar dodge once with a paranurse and kept her in a hallway for near to—"

"The lives and loves of Lieutenant Jolly will be continued next time," cut in Starbuck, tapping the big lieutenant on the upper arm. "While you're diverting those goons, Apollo and I'll sneak our viper ships out. If we're going to escort that ship to...to wherever it's going, we've got to be ready."

"Good luck to you," said Boomer.

"Good luck to you guys, too," said Starbuck. "Because when the flapdoodle hits the fan, we're going to be way out yonder. But you lads'll still be right here."

"True," said Boomer, laughing.

Starbuck leaned forward in the seat of his small viper ship and gazed down at the massive battlestar *Galactica*. He had his craft set in a hover pattern. "So far so good," he said into the voice pickup on his control panel.

Apollo's viper was hovering up above his in space. "This is only the overture," reminded his voice as it came out of a speaker grid.

"Aw, don't be so negative, sport," advised Starbuck, eyes on the yawning docking bay of the battlestar. "We haven't heard any whistles blowing, no alarms going off. Nobody's ordered us back. Therefore, I conclude this whole venture is off to a nifty start."

"I'm not negative, just practical."

"Go on," snorted Starbuck. "Gloom and doom is your middle name. Whereas me, I am always looking on the bright side. Take, as an example, the time we met that tattooed lady on—"

"Here comes the ship!"

Before Apollo finished the sentence the ship came rushing out of the dock, trailing flame and smoke. It shot free of the *Galactica* and went climbing swiftly away from the big space craft.

"I've always enjoyed fireworks," said Starbuck. "Shall we tag along?"

"After you," said Apollo.

"Okay, see you on...on wherever it is we're heading." Starbuck kicked his viper into action and went roaring off in the wake of the ship.

Councilman Geller had to take two deep breaths and clasp his right hand with his left before he could speak. "This is absolutely..." Words failed him.

"Outrageous?" suggested Adama. He was at a monitoring screen in his quarters.

"Outrageous and unheard of," said the angry fat man. "What exactly is going on?"

"The visiting ship has left us." The grey-haired commander turned away from the pictures coming in from the empty docking area.

"I know that, I know that." Geller's entire collection of chins jiggled. "How did it happen? I mean to say, there was a wealth of important information aboard that ship. The people, the equipment could have—"

"Somehow," said Adama, "the young man—Michael is his name, I believe—was able to return to his ship and take it out of here. I assume he's got it back on its original course."

"Am I correct in my understanding that he's also kidnapped a member of our medical staff, a young woman named Cassiopea?"

"I'm looking into the whole situation," Adama told him. "In a little while I'm sure I'll be able to answer all your questions."

"Well, this is all... outrageous. I mean to say, the Council has already voted that those people were to be revived and questioned," said the fat councilman. "But then you allow them to escape."

"Don't despair. We've been able to send two scout ships after them," explained Adama. "I'm certain we'll either bring that runaway ship back or follow it to its destination. Either way, we shall be able to learn a good deal about—"

"Those two scout ships," asked Geller, "who's piloting them, may I ask?"

"My son and Lieutenant Starbuck."

Geller pursed his lips. "Apollo and Starbuck, eh? That might not, meaning no offense to your parental feelings, be the best choice. Apollo is certainly capable, but that Starbuck does seem able to lead him astray and on previous—"

"I'm sure they'll do an admirable job," said Adama. "Besides, as I understand it, their ships were being readied for a routine patrol. Expediency dictated that they be enlisted in the pursuit mission. You can understand that, certainly."

Geller gave a reluctant nod. "I hope you won't mind if I conduct my own investigation into the entire deplorable situation?"

"Not at all," said Adama.

CHAPTER THIRTEEN

On the monitor screen Colonel Tigh's face showed slightly green. Even after fiddling with the controls, the commander couldn't get the faint green tinge to go away.

Giving up, he said, "Yes, go on."

Tigh said, "The concern is increasing."

"Understandably so," said Adama.

"And still no word?"

Adama shook his head. "The ships have been gone for nearly a secton and there's no news," he said, "no communication from Apollo or Starbuck."

"The Council is talking of conducting an inquiry."

"Oh, it's gone beyond talking, Colonel. I've been asked to appear before them."

"That might get rough."

"I'm sure it shall," agreed Adama. "At any rate, Colonel, I'll let you know as soon as I hear anything from out there." He broke the connection.

A speaker announced, "A young man seeking admission, sir."

"Who?"

"Boxey."

Smiling, Adama said, "Let him in, by all means."

The boy delivered a very careful salute when he was standing before his grandfather. "Boxey reporting for a briefing, sir."

Adama gave him a surprised look. "A briefing?"

"Well, all the kids have been wondering why we sent those children away," he said, rubbing at the floor with the toe of his boot. "Even Athena doesn't seem to be able to explain that. So I figured I'd come ask you, and she said that was okay so long as I didn't make an enormous pest of myself. But I told her that I never do that and that you like to see me and—"

"I surely do," said the commander.

"I kind of know why my dad and Starbuck left," the boy said. "It has to do, at least that's what Jolly told me, with keeping an eye on that ship that got away. I mean, that's duty. Except how'd we let them get away in the first place and especially the kids. It'd have been fun with a whole bunch of new kids to play with and all. There were four, right?"

"Four, yes," answered Commander Adama.

"So why did they?"

Adama looked away from the boy and out at the dark of space. "It isn't that easy to explain, Boxey," he said finally. "I know you are aware of a good deal of what goes on aboard the *Galactica* and—"

"That's because I'm naturally nosey," he explained. "Like Starbuck. Always poking my nose where it doesn't belong, that's what Athena says. Except, everything that goes on around here is interesting and I ought to know about it. So it isn't really eavesdropping or spying or—"

"No, it's what you call healthy curiosity." He held out his arms to the boy, inviting, "Come hop on my lap and I'll see if I can't...um...brief you, Boxey."

The boy hesitated. "If it's all the same to you, sir," he said in a muffled voice, "I'd like to sit in a separate chair. See, I'm not exactly a baby anymore and...well, officers and gentlemen don't sit on the commander's lap. Even if he is their grandfather. I bet my dad doesn't or Starbuck."

Adama chuckled. "True, Boxey. It has been quite a time since Apollo occupied my knee," he told the boy. "And the lieutenant never has. Very well, seat yourself in that chair there and we'll proceed."

"Aye, sir." Boxey got himself into an armchair facing the commander. "Ready when you are."

Steepling his fingers under his chin, Adama said, "Let me see if I can help you understand what's been happening. The people on that ship originally came from a planet known as Terra. They were—"

"That's just another name for Earth, isn't it?"

"Exactly, my boy," said the commander. "Originally people from Terra were sent out to colonize other planets that would help provide food and resources when those of Earth began to run out."

"But Athena told us these six people came from a place called Lunar Seven."

"They did, yes," said his grandfather. "The people we had as our guests aboard *Galactica* had apparently lived on an Earth colony called Lunar Seven from the time they were born. Perhaps their parents had lived there before them. What happened was, their bodies adapted to a lighter atmosphere. That meant they could no longer return to Terra and live comfortably. Nor could they adjust to our environment without considerable artificial help."

"Their air is different from ours?"

"It's something like diving deep under the ocean. The weight of all that water above you pushes down on you. Without the proper protection it can crush you," he told the listening boy. "Something similar takes place if you try to live in an atmosphere too dense for your body. Understand?"

"Sort of," answered Boxey. "So you let them leave so they wouldn't be crushed or hurt here on the battlestar?"

"That's the idea."

"And they're out there looking for a place where they can live?"

"That's it exactly."

"My dad and Starbuck went along to help them," he said. "We can be darn sure they'll find a safe place."

"We can," agreed Adama.

Starbuck yawned, blinked and straightened up in his seat. "How come I'm always slumbering when something important starts transpiring?" he asked no one in particular.

"Keep quiet," advised Apollo's voice out of the control panel speaker, "and listen."

There was another crackle of static and then the strange voice that had awakened Starbuck a moment earlier said, "Paradeen Control Center to Lunar Shuttle Avion. We have you on visual. Do you read?"

"This is Lunar Avion, responding. We have you on visual as well. All systems are operative and in stand-by mode."

"Very well, Lunar Avion. You are twenty hours behind your ETA. What is the status of your support system?"

"All well within tolerances to complete rendezvous satisfactorily."

"Very well. Stand by for further instructions."

As the crackling faded, Starbuck, after relighting his cigar, said, "Who was doing all that chattering?"

"We planted a transceiver in the control cabin of the ship, remember?" replied Apollo from his viper.

"I know that, old chum. But we didn't plant a guy with a deep furry voice," the lieutenant pointed out. "One of those voices was coming from our destination I conclude, but who was doing the talking on the ship?"

"Let's ask Cassie," suggested Apollo. "Cassie, do you read me?"

Silence flowed out of the speaker for almost thirty seconds. Then the young woman's voice answered. "I read you, Apollo."

"Aw, don't you read me, too, Cass?" asked Starbuck.

"Of course. Now stop interrupting."

"It gets lonesome out here in the vastness of space. I like to be remembered—"

"Starbuck, shut up. Now, Cassie, was that voice coming from your ship?"

"Yes," she replied. "It's the voice of the computer that's been flying this ship, which leads me to believe we're nearing our destination."

"Okay, we're still right on your tail," said Apollo. "Is everything okay aboard?"

"Things are fine," she said. "Although taking a trip with everybody else asleep isn't the most lively way to travel."

"I knew I should've stowed away on that crate," said Starbuck, puffing on his stogie.

"Just a minute, fellows," came Cassiopea's voice.

"Looks like Michael is reviving again. I'll find out what he has to say and get back to you."

"Yeah, do that," said Starbuck.

Michael glanced around the control cabin, then seated himself in a seat next to the one the young woman occupied. He scanned the panel of lights and dials in front of him. "Yes, everything is going smoothly. Our little stay with you people hasn't fouled anything up too badly."

"How do you feel? Should you be up?"

He laughed. "If the ship didn't think I should be, I wouldn't be, Cassiopea," he said. "The ship's already begun to adjust to the surface pressure of Paradeen, which is the planet we're aiming for." He flicked a toggle and a misty picture of a fast-approaching planet loomed to life on a view screen in the wall. "There she is."

"We'll be landing in how long?"

Michael read off several gauges and dials. "Exactly two hours and fifty-seven minutes from now. Yep, everything is going according to plan. I was to be awakened three hours out."

She sighed slightly. "I'm glad everything is functioning."

"You can communicate with the scout ships, can't you? I heard you when I came in."

"Yes, I can."

"I want to talk to Captain Apollo."

"Just talk, he's already hearing you."

A frown crossed his face. "Very efficient," he said. "Captain?"

"I hear you, Michael." Apollo's voice, a shade tinny, came from the transceiver unit that had been placed in the cabin.

"Okay, let me tell you that I'm in fine shape," Michael began. "Our ship is proceeding on automatic. The other voice you heard was from the computer on the former base we had on Paradeen. If you'll follow us down you'll be perfectly safe."

"Former base?"

"Far as I know there is nothing much left on Paradeen," said the dark young man. "Except Sarah's father. But there'll be a place for us and the children there."

"We can go into the details after we've landed."

"Yes, but I did want you to know one thing," said Michael. "One thing more, since it seems important to you. We've arranged to destroy the homing transmitter as soon as we're down. That's necessary in order to protect—"

"Wait now! Are you saying you're going to destroy the co-ordinates back to Lunar Seven?"

"There's no other choice. They may be following us already and so—"

"Cassie, stop him! Don't let him touch anything," ordered Apollo.

Michael made no move, simply smiling over at the young woman. "There's nothing you can do, miss," he said. "It's all being taken care of down on Paradeen, all automatically." He paused. "I'll be saving not only our lives but yours."

"From whom?"

"The Alliance," he said. "I've told you about them, but you don't seem to understand how dangerous they are."

From out of the transceiver came Starbuck's voice. "Nobody's asked me," he said. "But I just want to go on record as saying I don't much like this latest turn of events."

CHAPTER FOURTEEN

Elsewhere in space a huge dark craft was moving on its course.

Inside the ship a lean man of fifty, clad in a two-piece outfit of military cut, was moving slowly around a communications room. The greenish glare of the communicating and tracking screens was reflected on the gold braid that was thick on his chest and shoulders.

From across the room one of the men at a monitoring desk cleared his throat and then called out, "Commandent Leiter?"

"Yes, Krebbs?" He strode over to the heavyset young man.

"Concerning the small craft which escaped Lunar Seven six weeks ago, sir," said Krebbs.

"Ah, yes, our sister ship, Destroyer Two, reported the incident," said the lean commandent. "Nothing important as I recall. Some children, a farmer and a young girl were all who were involved." He rested a gloved hand on the black metal top of Krebbs's desk and glanced at the screen over the desk. "Has their ship entered our zone?"

Krebbs licked his lips. "I'm not certain, sir," he replied. "But my readout clearly matches the specifications and basic schematics for the ship that escaped Lunar Seven."

Stroking the thin scar that snaked along his left cheek, Commandent Leiter said, "How far away from us?"

"Twenty thousand kilometers, sir," answered Krebbs. "Apparently the craft is bound for the planet Paradeen."

"That's a long way off," reflected the officer. "Too far to go just to round up a few runaway children. We will, however, stop off there when we complete our patrol circuit. After all, they ought to be dealt with. Firmly."

"The thing that's been puzzling me, sir," put forth Krebbs in a somewhat timid voice, "is . . . well, there's more than one ship."

Leiter stiffened. "More than one, you say? That's not possible, is it? Our initial reports clearly stated that only a lone ship had made the escape."

"Nevertheless, sir." Krebbs reached out with stubby fingers to tap the greenish screen. "See those two dots there, in the wake of the larger dot?"

The commandent's eyes narrowed as he studied the screen. "Yes, they are definitely space craft. Have you determined what sort they are?"

"That's the problem, sir," said Krebbs. "I have never seen similar craft. And the analyzer has so far been unable to compute their method of power or planet of origin."

Leiter stroked the scar again. "That's impossible, Krebbs," he decided. "There can't be craft in this sector that we know nothing about. You've made a mistake."

The young man lifted several long streamers of print-out paper up off his dark desk top and rattled them. "The computer is never wrong, sir," he pointed out. "If you'll check over this data, you'll see I'm right."

Making a shooing gesture at the bundle of rattling paper, Leiter said, "Very well, I'll take your word for it." He took three steps back. "Whatever you do, don't lose contact with those two alien craft."

"Yes, sir."

"I'll go to the bridge now and inform them to alter our course for Paradeen," said the commandent.

"But we're due on Lunar Nine in three days, sir, and if we made a side foray to Paradeen the entire—"

"This is much too intriguing to pass by," he said, turning away and walking rapidly out. "Much too intriguing."

The smaller android was holding a bouquet of brilliantly orange flowers in his white plastic hand. There was a broad anticipatory smile on his white plastic face. "Boy, am I excited, agitated, wrought-up, all of a twitter, fervid, fervent—"

"Close your yap and hop on this dingus," suggested his companion, a larger android of similar design.

The two of them, each wearing a one-piece suit of pale yellow, were standing in the thin afternoon sunlight on a slanting field of pale blue grass. Parked next to them was a silvery hovercraft. In the nearby trees crimson birds sang in the interlocking green branches.

"Gee, Pop," complained the smaller android, "you're forever discouraging, daunting, disconcerting, disheartening and otherwise deterring me."

"Hector, I am not your Pop," said the larger mechanical man. "Nor am I your Mom, your uncle, your grandpappy or even your third cousin Freddy."

"But, gee, Vector," said the other mechanical man, lowering his head and poking a white plastic foot into the blue grass, "I wish you'd quit denying paternity. Makes me feel like a real—"

"I assembled you, dimbulb, and that's all I did," Vector explained. "Built you from spare parts lying around in the professor's lab. It was just something to do to while away the lonely reaches of the night. See? So there's no need to go all sappy and—"

"If you keep up this squabbling, Pop, we're going to be late for our reception committee duties."

The android made an exasperated sound inside his metallic nose. "Haul your scrap metal backside onto the hoverer then, dunce, and we'll get a move on."

"Ready and willing, Dad." Hector boarded the craft and arranged himself on one of the passenger seats. He crossed his legs and gazed up into the late afternoon sky.

After settling into the pilot seat, Vector inquired, "Do you have to sit like that?"

"Like what?"

"You look very much like a pansy, with your legs crossed and your hand on your hip."

"This is the way everybody sits. In a survey one hundred people were asked their favorite sitting pos—"

"Never mind." Vector, muttering, activated the controls.

The sled produced a low keening sound, then began to rise into the air until it had reached a height of some twenty feet.

"Whoopee," remarked Hector.

"Uncross your darn legs, beanbrain."

"I'm as masculine as they come, Pop." Hector sniffed deeply at the bouquet. "When you point out these imaginary flaws, though, it does make me feel low and causes distress, tribulation, woe, suffering, displeasure, dissatisfaction, malaise, vexation of spirit, palpi—"

"Quit babbling," advised the senior android while punching out a flight pattern on the control box. "I knew I shouldn't have used that double-strength vocabulary tube in you. What a dimwit thing for me to have—"

"Other fathers are proud when their kiddies display a gift of gab, Pop," Hector pointed out. "Another thing that bothers me is that you never play baseball with me like the other—"

"You're not a little boy, you're a full-grown android," reminded Vector as their hovercraft carried them, gracefully, downhill. "Androids don't play baseball."

"Sure, they do. On the TV monitor up at the house I just saw the Lunar Six Giants whip the Terra Five Blue Sox in a twinight triple—"

"Those are sports androids, lout, built just to entertain a gaggle of halfwitted baseball buffs. They have absolutely nothing to do with how—"

"You never take me to the circus either."

"There isn't any circus on Paradeen. All these dippy notions of yours are due to some faulty memory chips I had to use when I was constructing your alleged brain. Therefore, cease vexing—"

"These flimsy excuses don't fool me," said Hector. "I suspect that I'm an unwanted child. Didn't you and Mom want me?"

"You don't have a Mom, dimwit. I built you," said the senior mechanical man. "Now quit flapping your bazoo. There's Miss Sarah's ship yonder. We've got some very serious news to give her and I don't want you futzing up things."

"You forget how personable and charming I am, Pop," Hector said, taking another deep sniff at the flowers.

CHAPTER FIFTEEN

Cassie adjusted her breathing mask and stepped out into the thinner atmosphere beyond the ship. "So this is Paradeen?" she said quietly.

An android marched up and handed her a bouquet of bright orange flowers. "Welcome, Miss Sarah," he recited brightly. "It is with deep humility and inner satis—"

"Dimwit, she's not Sarah." Vector gave Hector a bonging nudge in the side.

"No, I'm Cassiopea," she corrected. "That's Sarah coming out of the ship now."

Smiling, Hector bowed to Cassie. "Cassiopea is a very charming name," he told her. "My name is Hector, also charming, and my revered father here is named Vect—"

"I'm not his father," Vector hastened to explain as he went hurrying toward Sarah. "We're not related in any way at all. How do you do, Miss Sarah?"

The blonde young woman smiled tentatively at him.

"Why isn't my father here to meet us?"

"I'll explain everything in full quite soon now," the senior android promised. "First, though, allow me to welcome the rest of you. You must be Michael."

Michael remained in the doorway of their ship. "I thought Sarah's father would—"

"All will be explained," said Vector.

"Ah, and here are the kiddies," said Hector. He gave Cassie the bouquet and then clapped his hands together. "You've grown a great deal, both of you. And where are the rest of—"

"Hey, don't do that," Starbuck told the android.

"Don't you like to be hugged and patted on the head, my little man?"

"I do, but not by machines."

Hector looked over at Apollo. "How do you feel about that, sonny?"

"You've got us mixed up with the children," Apollo informed him. "They're still onboard the ship. We, on the other hand, landed in our own ships and—"

"Holy Moley!" exclaimed Hector. "Invaders!" He drew a blaster pistol from the pocket of his garment. "Trying to pass as innocent toddlers. I thought there was something fishy when I smelled cigar smoke on this one's clothes. You have to get up pretty—"

"Beanbrain," called Vector. "Put that weapon away. These men are friends of Michael and Sarah."

Hector scrutinized the two of them with his plastic eyes. "They look shifty to me, Pop."

"Shifty or not, they're not invaders," said the other android. "And quit calling me Pop in front of people. It's downright—"

"Do you get to call your father Pop?" he asked Apollo.

"Not very often," admitted Apollo with a smile. "He, to be frank with you, isn't the type of man you call Pop."

"My father there thinks he isn't either," said Hector, slowly putting his gun away.

Michael climbed down onto the bright grass, frowning. "Vector, why are you androids carrying weapons?"

"Nothing to be alarmed about, Michael," the android assured him. "Now then, if—"

"But I want to know why."

"Well, Miss Sarah's father thought it best to arm us when the hostilities broke out. That's all over now so—"

"What hostilities?" the blonde girl asked him.

Vector made a calming gesture with his white hand. "Hostilities are over and done with," he said. "Nothing to fear any longer. We should, however, move to the ranch as soon as possible."

Sarah asked, "Why? If there's no danger, then—"

"Night is coming on, Miss Sarah," said Vector, glancing up at the late afternoon sky. "The temperature will drop quite low with nightfall."

"Is my father waiting at the ranch?"

Vector turned away. "Yes, Miss Sarah. You'll find him there."

A puzzled frown on her forehead, she said, "We'd better get the children."

"I'll help," said Michael.

"Suit yourself." She went climbing back into the ship.

Cassie suggested, "Let's both lend a hand, Michael. Four kids are going to be a handful."

She followed the dark young man into the ship.

Starbuck took a cigar out of his tunic, then remembered he couldn't smoke it with his breathing mask on. "What'd you say your name was, chum?"

Hector said, "My name is Hector. It's very close to the name of my father over there. He's Vector. I think that's nice when fathers and sons have similar names.

Although, it might be even dandier if I was called Vector, Junior. How does that strike—"

"This planet we're on," cut in Starbuck, using his unlit cigar as a pointer. "Whose colony is it, who does it belong to?"

"Terra. I thought everybody knew that. You must really be rubes not to—"

"Manners, peawit, manners," warned Vector. "These gents are our guests."

"Can I help it if we have stupid guests, Pop? I'm just trying to be—"

"Knock it off," suggested Vector.

Apollo was looking at the hovercraft. "Did Sarah's father design that, too?"

"Yes," answered Hector. "He was a very brilliant—"

"He *is* a brilliant man, you mean," said Vector, elbowing him in the side.

"Oh, yes. Is. To be sure," said Hector. "But, Pop, gee, we're going to have to tell Miss Sarah sooner or—"

"Later is when we'll tell her," said Vector. "For now button your yap."

"Yes, Pop."

The house was made of wood and glass, a one-level sprawling sort of place sitting in a clearing at the edge of a forest of blue and orange trees. The light of the declining sun hit the front windows and turned them a sharp black. Three yellow birds went flapping up off the flat roof as the hovercraft set down on a patch of blue grass.

The four children, completely wide awake after their long slumber, tumbled off the landed hoverer and went frolicking over the grass, laughing and shouting.

Sarah ignored the helping hand Michael offered her and stepped off unaided. "Where's my father?" she asked, glancing up toward the big house. "You told me he'd be here to meet us when—"

"Miss Sarah," said Vector, climbing free of the pilot seat. "He wanted to be here to meet you, but . . ."

"But what? Where's he gone to?"

Hector said, "That depends on your notions about the hereafter. Some sects, according to my data chip, believe in the existence of a—"

"Idiot!" said Vector. "We were going to break the news to her gently."

Sarah looked from one bland android face to the other. "He's dead? Is that what you bumbling gadgets are trying to tell me?"

Michael attempted to put his arm around her. "Easy now, Sarah."

She twisted free. "What happened? Why did he die?"

Vector pointed at a spread of yellow flowers a few yards away. "He's buried over there," he said. "We thought a simple stone marker was best. It says just John Russell Fowler and the date of his birth and the date of—"

"Oh, get out of my way." The blonde girl pushed the android aside and went running to the yellow flowers.

When Michael caught up with her she was kneeling next to a small flat stone. "I know this is rough, but—"

"Go away, you don't know anything," she said, starting to cry softly. "This is all your fault. You and my father and all you other scientists. Making wars and sending people off to the most godforsaken corners of the universe just—"

"He died of an illness, Miss Sarah," said the senior android, who'd come quietly over to them. "A rare virus that he couldn't fight. It was very fast and he didn't suffer that much and his last thoughts were of—"

"Platitudes and cliches," the young woman said, standing up. "Is that all he built into you?"

"He gave us feelings, too," insisted Vector. "I miss him, too, Miss Sarah, but there is nothing we can do. He told us to make things as comfortable as possible for you and the children. To forget him and think about—"

"Oh, yes, think about the future. One of his favorite notions. Don't live now, live tomorrow. And it never came, not for him, not for anybody." She made a sobbing noise, spun on her heel and ran to the house.

Michael didn't try to follow.

Lieutenant Jolly tugged at the tip of his moustache. "That's fascinating," he said to the auburn-haired girl who was sitting across the rec lounge table from him.

"Do you really think so?" asked Zixi, tapping her forefinger on the table top slowly.

"I do, yes," the plump lieutenant assured her. "You're a fascinating young woman and naturally everything you say is going to be fascinating."

She gave a small shrug. "I got the impression," she said, "that your mind was wandering once again."

"Well, I am sort of worrying about Starbuck and Apollo," said Jolly, "since there's been no word from them in quite a spell. But, even so, I took in every detail of your fascinating yarn about your grandmother and—"

"Grandfather," corrected Zixi.

"Right you are. Your grandfather and her . . . his pet owl."

"Eagle," said Zixi. "Gramps had a pet eagle."

"Of course he did," seconded Jolly, tugging at his

moustache. "As I say, I hung on your every phrase. Chuckling inwardly at the part where her...his owl... eagle bit off your cousin Max's left—"

"Cousin Maxine."

"Cousin Maxine, to be sure. Bit off her left ear."

"Right earring." ·

"Oh, that's better. I was envisioning the poor guy... poor girl wandering around with only one ear," said Jolly. "But only missing an earring isn't too bad."

"This particular one had a gem worth $100,000 in it."

"Oh, so? You should've mentioned that, Zixi. It makes your narrative far more—"

"I did mention it." She reached across the table to pat one of his plump hands. "But don't get the idea I'm offended by your woolgathering during my family anecdotes. I'm quite used to being ignored by all and sundry. Besides, I know you're deeply concerned about your missing friends."

"Starbuck and Apollo aren't missing exactly. They just simply haven't gotten around to communicating with the *Galactica* for some reason. Why any—"

"Hey, Jolly! We've heard from 'em." Lieutenant Boomer, grinning broadly, came hurrying up to the table. "Hello, Mitzi, excuse my horning in again, but—"

"Zixi," she said quietly.

"Beg pardon?"

"My name's Zixi, not Mitzi. But don't let that bother you. Go ahead and tell Jolly your good news."

"Is it good news?" inquired Jolly while the black lieutenant was seating himself.

"Sure is," replied Boomer. "The commander's received a communication from Apollo. Came in a few hours ago."

"They're okay?"

"As of a few hours ago, yep. And so is the ship with

our recent guests and Cassie aboard."

"That's absolutely great."

"They've reached, or just about had when they communicated with Commander Adama, their destination."

Jolly leaned toward him. "So where are they?"

"By now they've set down on a planet called Paradeen," answered Boomer.

"Catchy name," said Jolly. "Could be they'll find out some info about Earth there."

"Yeah," agreed Boomer. "The next message from them ought to be mighty interesting."

CHAPTER SIXTEEN

Starbuck was sitting close to the deep stone fireplace in the living room area of the large, sprawling house. He rubbed his hands together and looked away from the crackling fire. Out beyond the high, wide glass windows the day had died and there was nothing to see but a crisp blackness.

"Does get a mite chill here of an evening," he said, taking a few quick puffs at his cigar.

"It's dimbulb's fault," explained Vector, who stood straight near one of the dark windows. "I especially instructed him to reactivate all the heating units. Living alone for so many months, we've not needed any of the—"

"Gee, Pop, I wish you wouldn't bawl me out in public." Hector was passing out cups of a dark, steaming liquid.

Apollo and Michael were also in the living room area, each occupying a deep armchair. Cassie and Sarah could be heard in the dorm wing of the house trying to calm the four shouting, giggling children and put them to bed.

"This drink is Javine," Michael explained as he took a cup from the serving tray. "A beverage quite popular on Lunar Seven."

Sniffing his mug, Starbuck said, "Smells sort of like nearcaf."

Apollo took a sip, made a noncommittal face and settled back in his chair. "I'm curious as to why there are no other humans on Paradeen," he said.

"What did happen?" Michael asked Vector.

"It wasn't our fault," the senior android replied. "What happened was . . . the Alliance."

Holding his cup in both hands, Michael stared into it. "They attacked Paradeen?"

Vector said, "That was just after you departed from Lunar Seven. Their ships attacked, destroying most of the populace with chemical-biological weapons. Then they departed."

"The virus that killed Sarah's father," said Michael, "that came from them?"

"We believe so," said the android. "Although he lived for almost three weeks after the attack. We didn't go into the details in front of Miss Sarah, to spare her feelings."

Apollo sat up. "Why did they do it?"

"That's their style," said Michael with a bitter laugh. "Destroy the people only, leave the buildings and the land and the animals. Eventually they'll come back, at their leisure, and plant a settlement here. They're in no great hurry. These attacks are part of a vast, long-range plan of conquest."

"What we've heard of these Alliance gents so far isn't very positive." Starbuck settled crosslegged on the floor with his back to the crackling fire. "Who the devil are they?"

Michael drank a little of his Javine. He glanced up at

the fretted ceiling. "Terra—Earth, as you call it—was once a planet of many nations. But eventually there were just two sides, East and West. There followed a long, protracted struggle between the Eastern Alliance and the Western. A struggle over food, resources, spheres of influence. The usual stuff."

Apollo asked, "The West lost?"

"The war is still ongoing," said Michael, shaking his head. "But the East has been systematically destroying our satellite planets, the ones we'd established as food suppliers and potential colonies. We fled Lunar Seven for Paradeen in hopes of staying a few steps ahead of the Eastern Alliance." He shrugged and spread his hands wide. "That was naive. Eventually they'll probably destroy us all."

"And it's our own fault," said Sarah, coming into the room. She brushed a stray strand of blonde hair back from her forehead and crossed to an empty divan to sit. "Relying on the scientists, letting them pollute so much of Terra and then every other planet, we tried to—"

"Did you get the kids safely to bed?" asked Michael.

"Oh, yes, finally," she said. "They're safe tonight, but how long is that going to last? If the Alliance doesn't destroy us, then we'll probably invent something on our own that will."

"Your father was a man of science, Miss Sarah," reminded Vector.

She gestured at one of the black windows. "Look what it got him," she said bitterly. "A grave in the middle of nowhere. He never even lived to see his grandchildren."

"Sarah, the whole problem is a lot more complicated than you're making out," said Michael. "It isn't merely a question of science versus—"

"Yes, yes, I know," she said, standing up again. "I've heard all the arguments. Many times. Excuse me, I think

I'll turn in." Lips pressed close together, she walked out of the room again.

Watching her, Hector said, "Looks like our gala welcoming committee didn't cheer her up."

In the chilliest, darkest stretch of the night Sarah rose from her bed. Silently, in the darkness, she dressed, adding a heavy jacket to the clothes she'd worn earlier. She stood for a moment, fully dressed and listening, and then made her way out of the room.

Walking quietly through the still, dark house, she let herself out into the coldness of the surrounding night.

When Sarah was a hundred yards from the house, she clicked on the small flashlight she'd brought with her. She pointed the beam at the damp ground and began walking more rapidly.

The night wind came rattling through the woods, sharp and cold.

She'd covered nearly a half mile when she heard something behind her. Halting, she clicked off the light and the blackness closed in.

A twig snapped, leaves rustled.

Taking a deep breath, she turned to face whatever it was that was following her.

"No need to be frightened, Miss Sarah."

She turned the light back on and splashed its beam on the polite plastic face of Hector. "Why are you trailing me?"

He blinked. "Why, that's one of my duties," he replied amiably. "To look after and protect you. Since neither Pop nor I require sleep and since we aren't bothered by the cold, we decided to stand watch outside the ranch tonight. Pop himself is over on the other side of—"

"Very thoughtful," she said. "Actually, though, I don't need any protection at the moment."

"All part of the service. We take care of you and yours and thus—"

"I know," she said, reaching out to touch the android's arm. "Right now, though, I want to be by myself. I'd like to take a short walk. I'm hoping it'll help me sleep."

"Oh, we have pills, all kinds, to help you sleep," he informed her helpfully. "Red ones, blue ones, green ones. Your father left a whole array of—"

"I'm not too fond of pills or synthetically induced sleep."

"Yes, I can see where you might feel that way." Hector nodded his plastic head. "Well then, what say I accompany you on your walk? I'm great company, having been built to be highly personable. I'm chockfull of amusing anecdotes, bits of witty conversation, plus woodsy lore and pithy—"

"I'm sure you are," she said, showing a trace of impatience. "Thing is, Hector, I'd like you to do me a favor and allow me to go myself."

The mechanical man grew thoughtful. "That might be hazardous."

"Nonsense. I'm not going to walk all that far."

"Yes, but the woods are—"

"Keep in mind that you're supposed to be serving me."

"Yes, that's my main duty in life, but—"

"Fine. You'll be serving me amply by allowing me to be alone for just a spell." Smiling at him, she turned away and resumed her nocturnal walk.

"Well...I suppose it's allowable..." Hector stayed put and made no attempt to follow the young woman. "You promise not to get into any trouble?"

Sarah kept moving and didn't answer him.

• • •

Commander Adama frowned at the communications screen. He stroked his strong chin and then clicked the screen off. "What can that mean?" he said to himself as he began to pace the main room of his quarters.

"Councilman Geller to see you," announced a speaker.

"Just what I need," muttered the grey-haired commander.

"Beg pardon, sir?"

"Show the old boy in," said Adama.

The corpulent councilman came rushing in as soon as the door opened. "The Council isn't happy," he announced.

"They seldom are. Sit down."

Geller remained standing. "We are willing to overlook, for now, the high-handed way in which things have been managed thus far," he said. "However, we want more information on this planet Paradeen. Can it, for example, sustain life?"

"The atmosphere reports haven't as yet come in."

"Exactly." Geller coughed into his hand and set several of his chins to jiggling. "The Council was soothed when news from Captain Apollo finally reached us. Here was a new planet, here was a possible source of important information about Earth and—"

"I'm aware of how important Paradeen is to us all, Councilman."

"Are you?" Geller strutted a few steps and halted. "Then why haven't you presented us with a full report of conditions on Paradeen? And detailed information on what the residents thereof have to say about Earth, Lunar Seven and any other—"

"I've just now been trying to communicate with your vipers."

"And?" Geller rose up on his toes.

"I've been unable to contact either of the ships."

The hefty councilman sank down on his heels. "I'm afraid I don't quite understand," he said. "You told us that Captain Apollo had contacted you and—"

"That was just prior to landing on the planet."

"He hasn't reported since?"

"He has not," answered Adama. "When I, just now, tried to contact him I was unable to do so. It seems something's happened to the sending-receiving units in both viper ships."

Geller sank into a chair. "But that's dreadful," he said, sighing. "That could well mean trouble."

"Yes, it could," said Adama.

CHAPTER SEVENTEEN

Commandent Leiter entered the communications room and stopped just inside the heavy metal door. He stood there, absently stroking the scar on his cheek, and watched the men at the green-tinted screens. Then, the ghostly green light of the room dancing and flashing on his gold-braided uniform, he walked down to the screen being tended by the chubby young Krebbs.

"What's the latest on our enigmatic ships?" the lean commandent asked.

Krebbs licked his lips. "All three have now landed on the surface of Paradeen," he answered, straightening up in his chair.

Fingertips resting on the scar, Leiter nodded. "How long will it take a communique to reach Terra from our present location?"

"Two months, sir, and a few days."

"What if we use the lightwave relay station on Lunar Seven?"

"That won't be possible right now, sir."

"And why is that?"

"The relay station was knocked out by sabotage, Commandent," replied Krebbs.

"What's the matter with those idiots on Destroyer Two? They don't even seem capable of policing an insignificant colony like Lunar Seven." He put his hands on his slim hips and leaned his head back. "Very well, very well. Put me in touch with the bridge."

"Yes, sir." Krebbs's plump fingers punched at buttons and dots of light.

His screen was wiped clean and then it flickered, turned briefly purple and gave way to the image of a thick-necked man with close-cropped tawny hair.

"Yes, what?" demanded the man, an annoyed expression on his flat reddish face.

"Commandent Leiter wishes to speak to you," Krebbs informed him, voice tinged with smugness. He got up from his chair and bowed at it.

"Commandent Leiter? What does he—"

"I want you to carry out my orders, Flight Captain Disch." Leiter had seated himself in the chair and was smiling bleakly at the screen.

Giving him a grudging salute, Disch said, "Yes, sir. How can I be of service?"

"I want us to proceed full speed to Paradeen," said Leiter.

"Full speed? That'll put a serious strain on our fuel supp—"

"Full speed," repeated the commandent quietly. "How long do you estimate it will take us to reach the planet, Captain?"

"Twelve hours approximately," Disch replied, lips barely parted. "But, sir, at the rate we're burning fuel there's a good chance we'll—"

"That'll be all, thank you." He stood up and walked away from the angry captain.

Apollo, alone, roamed the morning woods. He'd awakened early, feeling vaguely uneasy, and decided to do a little solitary exploring of Paradeen. At least of the area in the vicinity of the house Sarah's late father had left for her.

The mossy ground underfoot was a deep golden color and the trunks of the highrising trees a deep blue. The early morning sunlight took on a bluish tint as it came slanting down through the twists and tangles of branches.

"Are we any closer to learning some answers?" he wondered.

The wars and the troubles they were trying to escape from were apparently just as frequent here, and on faroff Earth as well.

Dry leaves crackled off on his left.

Spinning, Apollo drew out his pistol.

"Won't do you a bit of good, sonny."

"Huh?"

Apollo's gun was tugged free of his hand by an unseen force. It went rising slowly upward, did a lazy loop and dropped back snugly into his holster.

"Impressive, ain't it?" A gaunt old man clad in a bedraggled two-piece white suit came tottering into view from between the blue trees. "Name's Kurtiz. Sometimes known as Kurtiz the Hermit. Who're you?"

Swallowing, Apollo answered, "Captain Apollo. How'd you do the trick with my—"

"Weren't a trick," replied the hermit, whose tangled white hair hung down to his narrow shoulders. "Merely a simple demonstration of low-level telekinetic powers. I'm plum full of odd abilities and knacks. That's what gives folks the notion I'm strange. Why're you on this planet, sonny?"

"Visiting," replied Apollo. "Matter of fact, what are you doing here? I was told just about everyone was wiped out by—"

"Baw, that ain't so," the hermit said. "Even them halfwit robots know that ain't so. There's quite a few survivors scattered hither and yon. I'm one of 'em and just about the most interesting of the lot, too. What brings you to Paradeen?"

"We came here with Sarah and Michael. She's the daughter of—"

"I know who she is, sonny."

"Okay, we tagged along to make sure they arrived safely."

Kurtiz made a dry chuckling sound. "I suppose you was aiming to go back to whereabouts you come from pretty soon?"

"Soon, yes."

The chuckling grew louder, shaking the old man's lean frame. "That there's going to be harder than you think."

Frowning, Apollo asked, "What do you mean?"

The hermit said, "Oh, you'll find out soon enough, sonny," and slipped away to vanish from sight among the tall trees.

Starbuck came strolling back toward the house. His cigar was unlit in his hand and there was a thoughtful expression on his face. "Morning, Hector, old chum," he said, slowing.

"Shall I serve breakfast out here?" asked the android, who was standing on the blue grass. "You can have snapjacks, scrambled—"

"Before chowing down," Starbuck said, "I crave a little conversation."

"With me?" Hector brightened. "Well, sir, that's very flattering, Mr. Starburst."

"Starbuck."

"Starbuck, of course. Very flattering, because Pop keeps trying to tell me I'm such a dimwit that talking to a blank wall is more illuminating than—"

"I was taking a stroll in the woods yonder," said the lieutenant.

"You should have asked me to go along, to explain the names of all the trees, shrubs and specimens of wild life."

"There's one specimen I'm particularly interested in," he said slowly. "I saw, at least I'm pretty darn sure I did, someone lurking in the brush."

"Oh, really? Were you frightened or—"

"Mostly I was perplexed. Because I'll swear that was a human being watching me. A female human being with very prominent red hair. When I tried to approach her, she took off. I lost her in the woods and bramble."

Hector's plastic head nodded up and down. "That certainly sounds like Queenie."

"Queenie?"

"She usually doesn't drift this far from the City," reflected the android. "Yet the young woman does seem to have a knack for sensing such things and I imagine she got wind of your arrival and—"

"City?" Starbuck put both hands on the mechanical man's shoulders. "What city would this be, Hec?"

"There's really only one City," answered the android, pointing to the east. "Lies some ten miles from here, sir."

"Who lives there?"

"Very few now. Only some squatters like Queenie and her friends," said Hector. "Not a pleasant bunch, I might add. The girl herself can be sweet, but...such a temper. Once she—"

"But who built the city, what size is it?"

"It's quite large and was constructed a few decades ago by earlier settlers on Paradeen," said the android. "An earlier conflict destroyed most of the dwellers and later settlers here have tended to shun the City."

"But the thing is a real city, with buildings and all?"

"Well, you couldn't call it a city if it didn't have buildings, could you? That's the kind of dippy question my Pop is always criticiz—"

"What I mean is, there are official buildings and libraries and all that? Places where records are kept?"

"Certainly." Hector nodded.

The lieutenant rubbed his hands together. "I want to see that city," he said.

"Oh, I don't know, sir. I don't think we could guarantee your safety there," said the android, a look of concern touching his plastic face. "Why don't you just stay here and I'll tell you about the City. Wouldn't that be—"

"Nope, I'm going to see it," said Starbuck. "If we're lucky, there'll be all sorts of material stored there. Stuff about Lunar Seven and Earth."

"Well, perhaps after breakfast I could fly you over it in the hoverer," offered Hector.

"The hell with after breakfast," Starbuck told him. "We're going right now, old chum."

"Right now?"

"You got it," said Starbuck, turning on his heel and running toward the parked hovercraft.

CHAPTER EIGHTEEN

She was waiting for him at the edge of the woods.

"Morning, Sarah," Apollo said, stopping beside her.

The blonde young woman didn't quite meet his eyes. "I wanted," she said quietly, "to talk to you. Alone."

"Sure," he said, leaning back against the bole of a tall blue tree. "Something wrong?"

She kicked at the grass at her feet. "Not exactly, no," she said. "What I wanted to suggest was . . . don't leave, Apollo. Stay on with us."

"That's impossible," he told her. "We're on a mission, searching for Earth. It could mean the difference between life and death for our people."

She looked up at him then, put her hand on his arm. "But you can't leave me here alone."

He smiled. "You're not exactly alone," he said. "You have your children. And your husband."

She shook her head. "Michael isn't my husband," she said.

"Huh?"

"My husband was killed on Lunar Seven, over two years ago," she answered. "Michael and I were forced together by necessity. He's a scientist, like my father."

"And your husband wasn't?"

"He was a farmer," she said. "A bright intelligent man, but interested in growing things and not in destruction and death."

"Doesn't seem to me that either your father or Michael are destructive," he said. "Obviously I never knew your father, but judging by what he left behind—"

"That's beside the point," she cut in, impatient. "I don't love Michael. I don't want to be left alone with him here on Paradeen."

Apollo asked, "Why is he with you at all?"

"I told you it was necessity." She shook her head, blonde hair brushing her shoulders. "My father needed someone to help hide us on Lunar Seven while he made preparations here. In return father made room for Michael and his little daughter."

"Only three of the children are yours, then?"

"Yes. Cindy, the smallest blonde one, is Michael's daughter."

"Well," said Apollo, "whatever you feel about him, it seems to me Michael sure lived up to his part of the bargain. He looked out for you and your kids on Lunar Seven. And, more important, he got you all safely here. Maybe you aren't aware of how he stood up for you, when you were our reluctant guests onboard the *Galactica*. He—"

"Yes, yes, I know. He's a wonderful person," she said. "Nevertheless, I don't want to spend my life with him. Living with him here in this house my father built."

Spreading his hands wide, Apollo said, "These are problems you and Michael have to work out."

"They could be your problems," she said. "You must realize what I'm saying. I'm fond of you and I think you—"

"Wait now, Sarah," said Apollo. "I'm flattered and all, but you don't know me and I don't know you. Now if you were telling this to Starbuck...well, he's got a different sized ego than me and he'd probably believe you could fall in love with him in ten minutes. I don't work that way and I think you're just clutching at straws. You don't like Michael at the moment and here comes Apollo. So you—"

"Do I strike you as that shallow? Some idiot kid who throws herself at the first—"

"Not at all," he said. "But you are, if you'll slow down and think about it, rushing this. We're not in love...which doesn't mean that in some other place and under other conditions we might not be able to fall for each other. Here and now, though, it's out and out impossible."

"If you did have time, though," she said hopefully, "then...."

"All sort of pointless, Sarah," he said. "We'll be leaving here in a day or so, heading home for the *Galactica*."

"Suppose you don't leave?"

He frowned down at her. "We'll leave."

Sarah said, "All sorts of accidents can happen."

Apollo took hold of her shoulder. "What are you talking about, Sarah?"

"Nothing," she said, pulling away. "It's just that... never mind." Turning away from him, she went running back toward the house.

• • •

Apollo met more of the survivors about an hour later.

Both Sarah and the hermit had hinted, fairly broadly, that it might be tougher to get off the planet than he was expecting. That decided him on getting down to where they'd left the vipers. He hadn't been able to find Starbuck at the house and Cassie had been more than busy getting the kids dressed and fed. So Apollo was heading to check up on the status of their ships by himself.

"Got to be careful dealing with Sarah from now on," he reminded himself as he walked rapidly down through the high grass.

Far overhead three large orange birds were gliding in lazy circles across the morning.

He'd been surprised to learn Sarah and Michael weren't married. He'd naturally assumed they were. Shows how easy it is to arrive at the wrong conclusion, he thought.

"She is an attractive girl, though," he admitted to himself.

But there wasn't any possibility he'd be settling down on Paradeen. That just wasn't the course his life was going to take.

Eventually maybe he'd settle someplace, but not now. Not until the fate of the thousands of people of the rag-tag fleet was settled.

"And maybe we're getting closer to some answers. This planet might—"

"Hold her right there, pilgrim."

Up out of the brush a few yards ahead of him loomed a big, wide young man. He wore a faded two-piece suit of work clothes and held a blaster pistol aimed square at Apollo.

Apollo stopped. "Am I trespassing?"

"You might be for all I know, since that word don't mean nothing to me." He came stomping closer. "You're one of them fellers come in them fancy ships down yonder, ain't you?"

"I am. Name's Apollo."

"I'm Sut Meadows," the large youth informed him. "Got a farm, me and my brother, 'bout a mile from here."

"You survived the Alliance attack pretty well."

Sut shrugged. "We're awful hard to kill," he grinned. "My Grandpap says it's on account of we got mighty tough genes. You figure as that's so?"

"That'd account for it, sure," he replied. "Look, I only want to go down and take a look at my ship."

"Don't blame you." Sut kept the gun pointed at him. "Seeing as what's happened to it. I ain't sure if it was the Morelands or not."

Taking a step forward, Apollo asked, "What's happened to it?"

"Best take a look," advised Sut. "I just did. Never seen so much fancy hardware. Yessir, must of really been something before it was all smashed up."

"Smashed?" Ignoring the gun, Apollo started moving again. He started running downhill.

Sut tucked his blaster away in his pocket. "I guess you ain't dangerous, pilgrim," he said, taking off after Apollo. "Hey, wait up."

Cassie walked away from the house, slowly and not really heading anywhere in particular. The midmorning sun was warm, the sky clear.

"Cassiopea," called Michael from behind her.

She stopped and turned. "I was thinking of having a small look around," she said.

He caught up with her. "I suppose that's safe."

"You seem upset about something," the young woman noticed. "It can't be the kids, because they're all in tiptop shape."

"No, it's Sarah," he said. "Has she been talking to you at all?"

"Not about anything too important."

He said, "I have the feeling she's been discussing certain . . . things with Apollo."

"Well, he's got a very sympathetic ear."

"She's not very happy," he said.

"You can't expect her to be," said Cassie. "Finding that her father was dead, after traveling all this way across space."

"There's that, sure," he said. "But mostly she's unhappy about me."

"Give her time to get used to Paradeen. Then your marriage'll get back on the old—"

"Sarah's not my wife," he said. "We should have cleared up that misunderstanding a lot earlier."

"What about the children? I thought they were—"

"Little Cindy is mine," he said. "The rest of the bunch belong to Sarah. Her husband was killed back on Lunar Seven. So was my wife." He turned away from Cassie, shoulders hunching slightly. "That's why I feel the way I do about the Alliance."

Nodding, she asked, "How'd you and Sarah get together?"

"Her father's idea. There was a—"

"Ahum." Vector had come walking up to them.

"What is it?"

"Excuse me for intruding, sir," said the android with a small bow. "I thought, however, I ought to inform you of something."

"Sure, go ahead."

After producing another throat-clearing sound, Vector said, "It's that ninny Hector. Well, actually Hector and your friend Lieutenant Starbuck. Although I'm certain it's basically Hector's fault, since he hasn't half the brains

I built into that nitwit skull of his."

Cassie asked, "What's happened to them?"

The mechanical man tapped his chest. "Noting their absence, I started using my built-in tracking devices on them," he explained with a slightly smug smile. "It appears they've gone to the City."

Looking from the android to Michael, Cassie said, "What's the City?"

"Not a safe place to go," answered Michael.

CHAPTER NINETEEN

Apollo stepped out of his viper ship and then leaned back against it. "Damn," he said.

Sut eyed him. "Pretty bad, huh?"

"Not only did they smash up a lot of things," he said, "but they also carried off some parts. So even if we can patch up this damage, we're still stuck."

"Well, sir, Paradeen ain't such a bad little planet," Sut pointed out helpfully. "Oh, sure, we get raided by them Alliance Destroyer ships now and then, but if you can put up with that, why—"

"No, we don't intend to settle here." He went striding over to Starbuck's viper. "We were damn fools not to post a guard last night. But I thought there weren't any people around."

Sut watched him climb into the cockpit of the second viper. "That one's pretty bunged up, too, ain't she?"

It didn't take Apollo long to confirm that. Dropping

to the ground, he said, "These Morelands you mentioned, Sut. Did you see them doing this?"

"Not exactly, nope." He dug one boot toe into the sward. "When I come to take a look, they was just sort of poking around. More curious than anything else."

"Did you notice if they took anything? Like parts and such."

"Fact of the matter," said Sut, "me and them don't get on all that good. They kind of suggested I mosey on and mind my own dang business."

Apollo walked over to the ship that had brought Michael, Sarah, Cassie and the children here to Paradeen. He noted that the door to the main cabin hung slightly open. "If they damaged this one, too, we really are in a fix," he said, opening the door wide.

Somebody had.

The central control panel had been worked on with a spanner. Dials were cracked, switches bent, gauges dented.

And again wires and tubes had been removed and weren't in evidence in the debris scattered on the cabin floor.

"Whoever did this really didn't want anybody to leave here."

He sat down in one of the cabin seats for a moment, drumming his fingers on the ruined panel. Then he got up and went back outside.

"I think I better have a talk with the Morelands," he said. "Can you show me where they live, Sut?"

Sut poked the ground with his toe again. "Well, sir, I can, sure," he said finally. "Thing is, I don't believe it'd be too smart to go calling on them."

"Nevertheless," said Apollo, "I'm going to drop in on them."

• • •

A city it was.

Block after block of it stretched away into the distance. The buildings were of glass and metal, many of them rising high into the midday sunlight. And all of them were grey with age and neglect, overgrown with twists and tangles of vines. The wilderness had long ago begun taking back the land the City had been built on. Weeds grew up thick through the cracks in the paving, grass was high in what had been small park areas.

"Desolate, isn't it?" observed Hector. "As well as forsaken, null, devoid, vacuous, abandoned and—"

"Yep, it's all of that," agreed Starbuck, chomping on his cigar.

"Well, I imagine you've seen enough." Hector had their hovercraft hanging in the air at the rim of the City. "Best not to do too much sightseeing on your first jaunt. No, so we'll head back for—"

"Land this crate, Hec," advised Starbuck.

"Land it?"

"Set 'er down," amplified the anxious lieutenant. "I want to take a good look around."

"Much safer from up here, sir, twenty feet above the ground," the android assured him. "Wouldn't be surprised if there were snakes and other creepy, crawly things waiting below to—"

"C'mon, Hec, don't tell me your pop programmed you to be chicken."

"I am fearless, sir. However, you mustn't mistake sensible caution for cowardice."

Leaning, Starbuck glanced down at the high grass and brush beneath the hoverer. "I might bust some essential portion of myself were I to jump from up here," he reflected. "Still, if you don't lower this rattletrap, I'm going to leap."

"You can't do that! Pop would chew me out for weeks on end were I to allow you to break your neck."

"Exactly. It's to our mutual benefit to land."

Hector's eyes clicked shut for a few seconds while he considered the matter. "Very well," he said, punching out a descend pattern on the control box. "You have to pledge to be as careful as you can. Don't attempt anything risky."

"Promise," said Starbuck.

The hoverer drifted down, landing gently on the ground.

From off a gnarled orange branch of a high tree a dark bird went flapping up and away.

"Ugly gent," remarked Starbuck.

"A carrion eater."

"Glad he's ignoring me."

Hector remained in the pilot seat, hands folded in his lap. "I imagine ten minutes will be plenty for your initial tour of the City, sir. Therefore—"

"Hec, I'm looking for information about Earth." Grinning, Starbuck hopped free of the landed hovercraft. "I want to locate the libraries, halls of records, official buildings and such like."

"All today?"

"Righto," he confirmed.

"The task of sorting through possible mountains of data, should any such still exist in this ruined metropolis, would take even a person of superior design and structure, such as myself, endless hours. How then—"

"Granted I'm nowhere near as slick as you," grinned the lieutenant. "Even so, I want to get me an idea of what's here. Obviously, if there is anything stored here, I'm not going to be able to sort it today. I mean, though, to get an idea of what the City does hold."

"It holds danger, peril, hazard, precariousness, jeopardy and—"

"What about these squatters you mentioned?" asked Starbuck, getting his stogie relit. "About how many are we likely to encounter while exploring hereabouts?"

"Too many."

Starbuck made a tell-me-more gesture with his left hand. "Give me some specifics."

"Well, Queenie travels with a band of young louts," said the android. "That gang numbers around ten, I'd imagine."

"Are they the only gang who haunt the City?"

Giving a metallic sigh, Hector replied, "Would that they were. No, I fear there are other clusters of ne'er-do-wells who make this ruin their home. All the more reason, sir, for making our stay as brief as possible."

"Okay, and the sooner we start, the sooner we can quit, old chum. So come on out of that crate and let's have us a look around."

"You want me to escort you, is that it?" Hector stayed where he was.

"Sure, you're going to escort me," said Starbuck. "You're the local boy and I'm the rube from the sticks. Now get a move on, Hec."

Hector gave another sign. "Very well, although I believe this entire expedition is foolhardy and . . . *awk!*" Both plastic hands came suddenly flapping up to smack against his chest. He stiffened, made a tinny gurgling sound and then slumped back in his seat. His eyelids make a loud click as they snapped shut.

Starbuck frowned. "What the devil happened to you?"

"Heck, that's easy to explain," said a voice behind him.

• • •

The long shed behind the house was thick with shadows.

"Of course I'm coming along," Cassie was insisting.

With the help of Vector, Michael was rolling the spare hovercraft out toward the sunlight.

"It isn't safe," he told her.

She patted her holstered pistol. "All the more reason why I ought to go along."

"If I might put in a word," said Vector as the hoverer reached the outdoors. "Mr. Michael is right. The City is fraught with dangers."

"And Starbuck is stuck there," said Cassie.

Michael said, "Vector knows a lot more about the City than I do. From what I gather, all sorts of drifters and misfits have taken up residence there."

"And from what I gather," the girl said, "there are also likely to be valuable records and sources of information there. A large city must've had a library and other—"

"There is a distinct possibility," said the android, "that all that sort of material was long ago destroyed. By vandalism or by the simple ravages of time. The City, remember, was built long ago and—"

"Yes, I'm aware of that," she said. "But I am also aware of why Starbuck went there. You simply aren't going to keep me from going to the place myself to see what's going on."

Michael said, "You could do more good staying here."

"To look after the children, you mean?"

"Yes, to help Sarah," he said. "I don't like leaving her alone. Apollo seems to have wandered off, too."

Cassie turned to the android. "You said you can track Hector. Can you also communicate with him, find out if they are in any trouble?"

Shaking his plastic head, Vector answered, "Unfortunately I haven't gotten around to adding such sophisticated touches to that dimwit, Miss Cassie. However, I'll check again and see if I can get a fix on his position." He touched one hand to his chest and his eyes snapped shut.

"I hope you understand," Michael said to the young woman, "that I'm not trying to boss you around, Cassie. It's just that I think—"

"Odd, very odd," said Vector as his eyes popped open.

"Where's Hector?" asked Cassie.

Vector's shoulders rose and fell. "I haven't the slightest idea," he admitted. "For some reason I've lost all contact with him."

CHAPTER TWENTY

The Moreland spread covered several cleared acres framed by thick forest. There were three low, domed buildings clustered together and then alternate fields of growing crops and grazing animals. In the half-acre nearest the ranch buildings the cornlike crop appeared to be stunted, the ears a dingy grey and swollen.

"Lost most of that," explained the uneasy Sut as they approached the ranch, "on account of the last raid. Something they dropped out of that there Destroyer ship just plain ruined the maize and—"

"Far enough!" warned a voice from the main house.

All at once a jagged line was cut in the dirt between them.

While the dust was settling, Sut said, "Like I told you, these Morelands ain't all that cordial."

Framed in the doorway of the dome house was a large,

broad-shouldered man of forty-some. His dark hair and beard were flecked with grey and he cradled a blaster rifle in his powerful arms. "Who's that outlander you got with you, Sut?" he called out.

"Well now, Joshua, his name is Captain Apollo and he'd sort of like to—"

"I want to talk to you." Apollo began shortening the hundred yards separating him from the watchful Joshua Moreland.

"Could of dropped one of you back where you was," Moreland pointed out, "and the closer you come the easier she's going to be."

Apollo continued walking toward him. "I didn't come here for a squabble, Mr. Moreland," he said evenly. "What I—"

"You shouldn't ought to of come at all," the big man told him. "You're tied in with them gadget men up at the place yonder. Bunch of you come here yesterday, where you got no business to be."

"I did arrive yesterday. I'm not going to argue as to whether we've a right to be on Paradeen."

Moreland was studying him through narrowed eyes. "You don't look like you hail from Lunar Seven at all," he concluded. "And you got to wear that dingus to help you breathe our air. There's something mighty different about you."

"It's going to take quite awhile to explain just who I am and where I came from." Apollo stopped a few feet from the armed man. "Right now, I want to talk about my ships."

"Best thing you could do, stranger," said Moreland, swinging the barrel of the blaster rifle up so it pointed at his chest, "is climb in that ship of yours and hightail it off this planet."

Apollo laughed. "C'mon now, Moreland, you know

damned well I can't do that. Because my ship, along with the others, has been sabotaged."

"Has it now?"

"I have a hunch you know how the damage got done," said Apollo.

"You accusing me and my wife of breaking up them ships of yours?"

"You were up there this morning," said Apollo.

Gesturing with his rifle barrel, Moreland said, "So was Sut."

Apollo nodded. "Are you saying you didn't smash the control panel and take away some of the parts?"

"Ain't saying anything, stranger," said Moreland. "But I might just point out that I want you and them other fools to get the hell off Paradeen. Smashing your ships ain't going to help that none."

Rubbing his hand across his chin, Apollo said, "You've got a point."

"Why don't you tell him the truth," said the lean woman who appeared in the doorway behind Moreland.

Without turning he said, "This ain't no concern of yours, Annie."

"Why isn't it? If the Alliance comes back and attacks again, we may not be so lucky as we were last time," his wife said, stepping out of the shadows and looking at Apollo. "Your being here is only going to bring trouble."

"That's not my intention," said Apollo. "We came here to get information. If our ships hadn't been sabotaged, we'd have left in a few days."

The woman said, "Even a few days is too long. The Alliance knows what goes on here; they know everything. They must know there are strangers on Paradeen and they'll come here to take care of you. That'll mean trouble for us, too."

"Her brother was killed on the last raid," added Moreland.

After watching the woman's lined face for a few seconds, Apollo said, "You know who tried to wreck my ship, don't you?"

She averted her eyes and didn't answer him.

"Go on back inside, Annie," her husband urged.

"If I can find out who did it and what happened to the parts that were taken," said Apollo, "I'm that much closer to repairing my ship. You can see that, can't you?"

"Will you take all of them away with you?" asked Moreland. "That blonde girl and her kids, too?"

"Their home is here," he said. "I can't speak for them."

"Trouble," said his wife. "That's all it's going to mean. Trouble for all of us. As if we ain't had enough already." She began, softly, to cry.

"Go on inside," said Moreland, his voice not quite so harsh this time.

Without a word, his wife returned inside the house.

"You best get out of here now," said Moreland.

"You could help me by telling me what you—"

"Mister, I don't know a goddamn thing," said Moreland, prodding the air between them with his rifle. "Except this. When the trouble starts you are on your own. Now get."

Apollo took a slow breath in. He nodded once and went walking away from the ranch house.

"This isn't the kind of guided tour I had in mind," remarked Starbuck.

"Humdingers! I never have run into anybody quite like you," said the red-haired girl who was herding him along a damp, chill underground tunnel far beneath the City.

"There isn't anybody like me in the whole damn universe," he assured her as he stepped around a greenish puddle of muck. "I wonder, Queenie, if you could raise the barrel of that quaint blaster of yours a shade higher. I'm fearful you'll wear a hole in my kidneys."

"How in the heck'd you know my name?"

"Hector, my faithful android companion, told me," replied the lieutenant. "That was shortly before you fried his inner workings. How'd you do that anyway?"

"Shucks, he's not wrecked none," said Queenie, prodding him higher up on his back with her gun. "I merely temporarily turned him off."

"How?"

"Humdingers! I don't exactly know," she answered impatiently. "It's just a knack I have. By concentrating on little tricks like that I can make machines and such quit working."

"You must have some kind of psionic power." He glanced back over his shoulder at the slim redhead. "With a gift like that you could do great things."

"Heck, I'm content where I am," she answered. "What's your name anyway?"

"Starbuck."

"I thought so."

"What do you mean?"

"Ever since yesterday a couple or so names been running around up in my head," explained Queenie. "Starbuck, Apollo . . . Michael. I had this burning hunch new people was roaming around in the vicinity. So I went scooting out of the City to take a gander. I spotted you this morning. Would you say you was the cutest of the bunch?"

"By a long way, sure," he said. "Where are you taking me?"

"You're my prisoner," she said. "See, we don't like

strangers nosing around our city."

"How many of you are there?"

"Quite a few," she said evasively. "More than plenty to lick you and all your buddies."

Starbuck stopped and turned to face the girl. "How old are you?"

There were only a few globes of light along the long shadowy tunnel. They'd halted in a spot where there was little illumination and the girl's face was lost in darkness.

"I don't know exactly," she answered. "Not important anyway."

"Seventeen or eighteen, I'd guess."

"I've been here ten years and I had to of been more than eight when I got here."

"Got here from where?"

"Someplace else," she said. "Why the heck are you asking me all this stuff for?"

"For one thing, Queenie, I'm interested in you," he said. "For another, I'm hoping you can help me."

She laughed in the darkness, her small even teeth flashing suddenly. "I'm not about to help you out, Starbuck. Even though you are sort of cute and interesting," she told him. "Interesting, that is, compared to the usual line of fellows I run into."

"You've lived in this enormous ruin for a decade, okay. You must know where everything is, right?"

"Well, sure I do. Humdingers! I'd be pretty stupid if I didn't," she said. "And I probably wouldn't of survived if I didn't know my way around darn good."

"Right, exactly," he said. "So you're the perfect one to help me find what I'm looking for—the sources of information in this burg. First I want a library, the biggest one you've got. Then—"

"Doesn't matter what you want, Starbuck," she explained. "You don't have any say."

"Aw, you're not going to remain loyal to some kid gang, Queenie," he said. He gestured with his cigar at the low, slimy roof of the tunnel. "Paradeen is but one planet in a universe full of planets. There are worlds and worlds out there in space. Full of wonders."

"We got wonders enough right here." She poked him in the ribs with her gun. "Get moving again, please."

"You help me and I'll see to it that—"

"Is this guy giving you trouble, Queenie?"

"No, Scrapper."

A large young man had stepped out of the shadows up ahead. Most of him was flesh and blood, but his right arm was made of dented metal. "Taking you a hell of a long time to get him to the den," he said in his low raspy voice.

"That's entirely my fault," said Starbuck. "I insisted in being shown all the high spots along the way. This is a very fascinating sewer and naturally—"

"Just shut up," said Scrapper.

Starbuck looked him up and down. "You know, chum, it's just possible that you and I aren't going to get along."

Scrapper said, "That don't make any difference, buddy. You won't be around long enough for it to matter."

"Oh," said Starbuck.

They were gathered around the hovercraft when Apollo came hurrying back toward the house. "Something wrong?" he asked.

"Looks like." Cassie came over to him. "Starbuck and Hector apparently took off to explore a city that—"

"There's a city around here someplace?"

"So I'm told," she replied. "When Starbuck heard about it, he persuaded Hector to take him there in the other hoverer."

"And something went wrong?"

"We think so. There's been no word."

"Is he likely to get in trouble there?"

"There are several gangs of lowlifes who inhabit the City," Vector informed him. "Hector should've known better than to—"

"Damn, this planet turns out to be less uninhabited all the time," said Apollo, slapping at his thigh with his palm. "Okay, we better get over and take a look at this city."

"The reconnoitering has to be carefully done," cautioned the android. "I don't know the fate of Lieutenant Starbuck, but I can tell you that Hector has ceased to function."

Apollo moved nearer the hovercraft. "Let's go," he said to Michael.

Michael asked him, "Where have you been? You looked angry before we even told you about Starbuck."

"Yeah, I've been chatting with some of your neighbors," Apollo said.

"Neighbors?" Cassie was puzzled. "You mean there are—"

"Oh, there are quite a few of 'em," answered Apollo. "Most of 'em not too friendly."

Michael frowned. "Maybe the best thing would be to just stay clear of them."

"I was after a little information," said Apollo. "Mostly I wanted to find out who smashed the controls of our ships."

Cassie made a gasping sound. "Apollo, you can't be serious?"

"Wish I wasn't, Cassie," he said, shaking his head. "As of now, there's no way of getting off Paradeen."

"You could use our ship," suggested Michael. "To get you back to your battlestar and then you could send it back some—"

"These vandals of ours were very thorough," Apollo told them. "They wrecked your ship, too."

"Can it be repaired?"

"In time and with luck maybe," said Apollo. "We might be able to patch up all three craft. The thing is, somebody also made off with some of the parts. That's going to make things even rougher."

"Why would these neighbors of ours do that?" asked Michael, looking at the android.

"I don't understand," said Vector. "The Morelands were never friendly, even when Miss Sarah's father was alive. They're very anti-machine in outlook, but they've never resorted to out and out damage."

Apollo said, "I'm not sure it was them who did all this."

"Who else then?" asked Cassie.

"We can talk about that later," he said. "Right now let's go see what sort of mess Starbuck's gotten himself into."

CHAPTER TWENTY-ONE

There were five of them in the underground room.

Starbuck never did learn all their names.

"Here he is," introduced Scrapper, giving him a shove that propelled him over the threshold and caused his dead cigar to pop out of his mouth.

Three of them were young men; two were young women. Most of them smiled on seeing Starbuck come stumbling into their meeting place, but not in ways that seemed cordial.

"Pleased to meet you," he said. "Let me explain how you can help out. First, I'm looking for...oof!"

"What did I tell you about keeping quiet?" Scrapper hit him again in the back with his metal fist.

The second blow sent Starbuck smacking into the nearest wall.

"Don't hurt him too much," urged Queenie.

"Why not?" growled Scrapper.

"Because," said the redhead, "he maybe knows lots of interesting things. We can learn stuff from him."

They were in the basement of what must once have been an office building. Old dented filing cabinets were stored here, festooned now with spiderwebs. A broken computer terminal lay on its side near a scatter of ancient office chairs.

Starbuck leaned against a battered desk. "Look, folks," he said. "I'm not here to make trouble. As Queenie pointed out, I can be of help to you."

"That seems highly improbable, old chap," a bald-headed youth in a one-piece green worksuit told him. He was crouched next to a nest of wastebaskets.

Starbuck continued. "You're not the only gang that haunts this city, right?"

"Ain't you never going to pay attention?" Scrapper raised his fist. "I want you to keep shut up till—"

"Let him talk." Queenie rubbed her fingertips along the side of her head. "I got the feeling he can help us in fighting some of our rivals."

The bald youth snorted. "Dubious at best, child."

"Let him mouth off awhile anyways," suggested a fat girl who sat in a swivel chair with a blaster pistol resting on her broad lap. "We can kill the slug soon as he gets boring."

"We don't have to kill him at all." The red-haired girl eased nearer to him. "Go ahead, Starbuck, talk."

"Okay, if you're through debating my future," he said. "As I was saying, dear friends, I come not to—"

"This bird's near as windy as you are, Big Words," observed a bearded young man.

"Hardly, old chap," said the bald youth.

"The thing that'll give you an edge," continued Starbuck, "is weaponry. That's true in any sort of conflict. Now, ladies and gents, I happen to have arrived on your fair planet, the pearl of the universe as I like to think of it, with a shipload of the latest stuff in weapons. State of the art, if you know what I mean."

"Malarkey," said the fat girl.

Starbuck pointed at Scrapper. "This gent took charge of the pistol I was carrying," he said. "Look it over, folks, and then try to tell me it isn't superior to the venerable junk you've been depending on."

"Perhaps we'd better take a close gander at the bloody blunderbuss," suggested Big Words, idly holding out a hand toward Scrapper.

Reluctantly the leader drew Starbuck's pistol from his belt. "Here. It don't seem all that great."

"If you'll allow me to demonstrate the distinct advant—"

"We aren't that dumb," the fat girl told him. "You take the gun and use it on us."

Starbuck tried to look shocked. "Wow, that's what I get for lending a helping hand," he said. "Okay, examine it on your own. Just be careful you don't blow your respective or collective brains out with it."

Big Words was holding the gun close to his face. "Ah, yes, it is of rather smart design," he muttered. "Considerably more settings than anything we've been accustomed to."

"On the lowest setting," said Starbuck, "you can deliver merely a mild shock."

"Who wants to do that?" asked the fat girl, causing her swivel to squeak as she shifted her bulk to get a better look at the gun. "We want to fry every slug who's not on our side."

"There are times," said Starbuck, "when stunning is wiser than frying, young lady. For instance, you take—"

"Keep still for a minute," advised Scrapper. "Big Words, what do you think? Is he full of crap?"

"On the contrary, old chap, this weapon is of decid-edly superior workmanship. I'd venture to conclude that a goodly supply of these would give us a distinct ad-vantage over our foes."

Nodding, Scrapper nudged Starbuck. "How many more you got?"

Starbuck grinned. "How many do you need, old chum?"

Colonel Tigh said, "Frankly, sir, I don't know exactly what to make of it."

The commander was sitting in an armchair, going over the sheaf of data sheets the colonel had brought him. "We have to assume, judging from this," he said, "that the communication units in both vipers have been delib-erately destroyed."

"Yes, that much seems clear." Tigh was sitting on the edge of his chair, watching Adama. "Our probe instru-ments, of course, aren't sophisticated enough to give us any specific details. Not at this remove from Paradeen, at any rate."

Resting the sheets on his knee, Commander Adama steepled his fingers beneath his chin. "We can also con-clude that there's been some sort of trouble involving both Apollo and Starbuck."

"There's no way of determining the nature of the trouble."

Adama picked up the papers again and leafed through them. "I'm also concerned about this part of your report, Colonel," he said, tapping a paragraph in midpage. "Can you give me any further details?"

"Again, sir, we're at too great a distance for detailed information," answered Tigh. "All we know is that a large alien space craft seems to be heading for Paradeen."

"Cylon?"

"No, that much we're sure of."

Thought lines formed on the commander's broad forehead. "Who then?"

"That we don't know," said Tigh. "I'd venture to guess that whoever it is might mean more trouble for Apollo and Starbuck."

Gathering up the data sheets, Adama stood. He crossed to his window and gazed out into the immensity of space. "Thank you for bringing this to me," he said finally.

"Are we to take action?"

"Not yet."

"But—"

"Yes, I know," said Adama. "But I believe we have to give them more time. If I change my mind, I'll contact you."

"Very well, sir." The colonel rose up and left the commander's quarters.

A moment later a speaker announced, "Councilman Geller to see you."

Scratching his chin, Adama replied, "Tell the councilman I'm not at home."

CHAPTER TWENTY–TWO

"Humdingers!" said the red-haired Queenie in an unhappy voice. "I shouldn't ought to be doing this."

"Aw, a short side trip isn't going to matter," Starbuck assured her.

The two of them were making their way along a narrow underground passway, one that branched off the larger tunnel the girl had guided him through earlier. The stone walls were damp, streaked with purplish mildew, and the sound of dripping water could be heard off in the shadows.

"You're darn lucky," said Queenie.

"Meeting you, you mean?"

"I mean being able to con Scrapper and Big Words and the rest of 'em," she told him. "All that guff about bringing back all sorts of guns for them."

"Would I tell an untruth?" he asked innocently as he followed her over the damp stone walkway.

"Tell 'em you'll get 'em guns and I'll go along to see you come back with the stuff," she said disdainfully. "You plain forget I got me a few extra knacks, Starbuck. I pretty often get awful strong hunches about what folks are thinking."

"Got to be careful with a gift like that."

"The point being, I got an awful good notion you came up with this scheme just to get yourself out of a jam."

"Me?"

"On top of which, I was scouting outside the City," she continued. "Been doing that since you arrived on Paradeen."

"That's good, travel is always broaden—"

"I *saw* your ships, Starbuck. They ain't what I'd call loaded up with guns."

He slowed, shrugging one shoulder. "With all these suspicions, why'd you agree to go along and keep guard over me?"

"Because . . . well, I don't see any sense in letting 'em kill you," Queenie said quietly. "Although I'm going to be in real trouble when I get back without one single new gun or anything."

Starbuck said, "You don't necessarily have to go back."

"Oh, so?" She laughed. "I sure ain't going to live out in the woods from now on, like that old coot Kurtiz the Hermit."

"Haven't had the pleasure of meeting the gent, but there are other places to live," he said. "Our friends Michael and Sarah could put you up. Or we might be able to squeeze you in one of the vipers and transport you back to our battlestar. A battlestar, in case you're wondering—"

"Is a viper what you call those dinky ships you came here in?"

"That's right. And a handsome name for a—"

"Climb up on that." She pointed at a metal ladder they were approaching. "It'll take us to the street level."

"Okay, sure." He took hold of one of the rusty rungs and started climbing upwards. "Why were you asking about our vipers, Queenie? I detected an odd note in your voice."

"I was over there, having me a look," she said as she followed him up into the shadows. "Middle of the night it was."

"And?" He jerked his head back when a fat white rat went scurrying along a ledge he was passing.

"Saw somebody messing around. . . . Push up on that hatch above you."

He complied and the metal trap door lifted. Starbuck pulled himself up into a small, grey-walled room. "You saw somebody tampering with our ships?"

Queenie ignored the helping hand he extended, boosting herself into the room unaided. She then dashed across it to a dusty round window and stared out. "Looks okay outside," she announced. "The dang library you're so anxious to poke around in lies right across the street. I'll doublecheck that it's safe outside and then we'll run for it."

He caught her slim arm. "First finish telling me about our ships."

"I saw somebody smashing the works with a wrench," the redhead answered. "A blonde woman it was, sort of pretty."

Starbuck's mouth dropped open and all he managed to say was, "Huh?"

"She banged up the controls in both your vipers or whatever you call 'em," Queenie went on. "Then went in and messed up the control panel on that bigger ship."

He shook his head. "That blonde girl must've been

Sarah," he said, puzzled. "But why in the devil would she do something idiotic like that?"

"Well, if you ever get back to her, you can ask," said the girl. "Right now, though, let's concentrate on avoiding the rival gangs and getting you inside that stupid library."

"I don't sense a trap," whispered Vector.

The search party was crouched in the brush near the edge of the City. In the waning light of the late afternoon they could see the other hovercraft and the other android slumped in the pilot seat. A half-dozen small yellow birds were hopping around on the hoverer and another was perched atop Hector's plastic head.

"No sign of Starbuck," said Apollo.

"We'd best," suggested Vector, "move ahead and investigate."

Nodding, Apollo tapped Cassie on the shoulder. "Stay here and back us up in case something goes wrong."

"Will do," she said.

The yellow birds went scattering up into the new twilight, the one on the android's skull taking flight last.

"Hector?" said Vector, reaching up and tapping his mechanical colleague on the chest.

There was no response.

Circling the craft, Vector climbed aboard and sat in the front passenger seat.

"Ground's trampled all around here," noticed Apollo. "Somebody besides Starbuck was here. Looks they headed into the City together."

"Don't be stubborn now, Hector," the android was saying. "If you can talk, talk."

Silence.

Giving a rattling sigh, Vector reached in and opened a compartment in his side. From it he drew out a small compact tool kit. "I believe I can fix him in a jiffy," he said confidently. "My guess is someone used a disabling beam on the poor lad."

While' Vector tinkered, Apollo scrutinized the area around the hovercraft. There was a definite trail to follow here, but he was near certain it would die once they reached the City itself.

Who the heck had grabbed Starbuck? And why?

If they'd just wanted to murder him, they'd have done that on the spot. But there was no evidence of bloodshed or even a scuffle.

"These gangs that roam the City," he asked Vector, "would they be likely to kill Starbuck?"

"They'd kill anybody," replied the android. "That's why it was highly thoughtless of Hector to—"

"Gee, Pop," said Hector as his eyes popped open, "you're forgetting that I am designed to aid humans. Therefore, albeit reluctantly, when—"

"Do you have any idea what happened?" Apollo came up close to the repaired and revived mechanical man.

"Of course. I have a crystal-clear idea of all that transpired. Because, you see, although I was incapacitated and unable to move, my sensory equipment continued to function. I couldn't aid the lieutenant, yet I saw and heard all that went on."

Apollo asked, "What happened?"

"A red-haired girl," answered Hector.

"Yep, that sounds like something that'd happen to Starbuck," said Apollo. "Details?"

"She was lying in wait for us," Hector recounted. "Lieutenant Starbuck had stepped off the craft and I was about to. Then, without warning, a strange feeling swept over me. I was all a-flutter, filled with—"

"Quit embroidering the story," said Vector. "Just give us the facts."

"I can't help it if I give facts in a colorful way, Pop," said Hector, pouting slightly. "After all, if you hadn't wanted me to be glib and—"

"Never mind. Get on with it."

"That's what I'm trying to do. At any rate, this girl did not, I'm willing to swear, use a weapon on me," he said. "No, I do believe the lass is possessed of psi powers. That she's able to put the whammy on a highly complex mechanism simply by willing it. Well, be that as it may, she surely put some sort of whammy on me. I was paralyzed, stiff as a board. Well, not exactly a board, since I went limp like a noodle. Anyway, while I was in that state, she appeared in the clearing here and pointed a nasty looking pistol at the lieutenant. He tried to be glib and charming, but she was having none of it. Although I did sense she found him charming. The problem was, she was on orders from others. A clear-cut case of love versus duty, which we so oft see in—"

"She took Starbuck?" asked Apollo.

"Led him away to their lair," answered the android.

"Were they planning to kill him?"

"It's my impression they wished to question him first," said Hector. "After that. . . ." He shrugged.

Apollo said, "Any idea where this lair of theirs is?"

"I should be able to use my sensors to get a fix on where Lieutenant Starbuck is at the moment."

"Okay, do that," said Apollo. "Michael, you stick here to see that nobody sabotages our hovercraft. The rest of us'll go hunting for Starbuck."

CHAPTER TWENTY-THREE

The place was immense—a huge dome of a building with ramps and rows of shelves rising up all around and crisscrossing.

"This is a library, sure enough," observed Starbuck, gazing up at the tiers of books. Slowly and thoughtfully, he took out a cigar and lit it.

"Find what you want and let's get clear of here," urged Queenie, glancing back anxiously over her shoulder. "This is pretty much Commando territory. We don't want to linger."

There was dust thick on everything and the high, round windows let in little of the thin twilight. The smell of mildew and decay was strong, and sprawled on the floor were tumbles of books and readspools and papers. Near the foot of one of the climbing ramps, someone, long ago it seemed, had built a bonfire of books and papers.

After taking a puff of his stogie, Starbuck asked, "Who're the Commandos?"

"Another gang," she said. "A lot nastier than any of us."

Starbuck started up the nearest ramp. "Doesn't look like they hang out here much."

"Nobody likes this place," the red-haired girl said, following. "Some of them figure it's maybe . . . sort of haunted."

"Good," said Starbuck, grinning. "That way they're less likely to come barging in."

"The Commandos'll come in if they get wind we're poking around in here."

"I'll hurry," he promised, striding toward a catalog area.

The three squat rows of file cards were decked with spider webs and dust. Three chittering black mice went scurrying out from between the rows as he approached.

"Your Commando buddies don't keep up their buildings too well."

"I told you they never come in here unless . . . unless it's important," said Queenie. "And killing us'd be important to those louts."

"I was merely making a quip," he explained, brushing the dust and webbing off a cabinet. "To lighten the mood of things."

"Nothing's going to lighten my mood except getting out of this place."

"Soon," he said. Narrowing his eyes, Starbuck tried to make out the inscription on the file drawer. "DAV to HOB. Then Earth must be in this drawer." It took two strong tugs to get the drawer open.

A mouse leaped free, trailing a confetti of file cards.

"Damnation," said Starbuck, "these critters've been

munching on the file cards. What a way to run a library."

"What's so all-fired important about Earth, anyhow? I never heard of the place."

"We want to find it," he said as he flicked through what was left of the cards in the musty drawer. "To settle there maybe."

"You and your friends?"

"Me and several thousand others," he answered. "There's a whole fleet of ships out there."

"Humdingers!"

"Ah, they didn't eat all the cards pertaining to Earth. Yep, according to these there are books on the subject on level 12ES." He stepped back and looked up. Level 12ES ought to be up in that direction, huh?"

"I suppose," answered Queenie without much enthusiasm. "But why don't we come back tomorrow or the next—"

"C'mon, we'll find the books now and get away," he said, starting up another slanting ramp. "Never put off to tomorrow what you can do today, Queenie. Especially if it looks like you may get knocked off before tomorrow."

"That's not funny," she told him. "Making jokes about being killed."

"Who's joking?" He was walking fast.

"I never have encountered anyone like you," she said, tailing along.

"I'm unique," he explained. "One of a kind. In fact, I've been thinking of approaching an android manufacturer and seeing if they'd like to turn out replicas of me. I think they'd sell like hotcakes."

She snorted. "There aren't enough halfwits in the universe to make selling replicas of you a going business."

"Hey, Queenie, I thought we were friends."

"Well, we are. Sort of, but my fondness for you has been going down lately," she said. "Ever since you talked me into coming in here."

"Now I'm not up on the way diplomacy works on Paradeen," he said, "but it seems to me you folks ought to be able to get together and work out your differences. You and the Commandos and the other gangs who—"

"Oh, sure," she said, laughing, "the way you've worked out your differences with the Cylons."

He frowned back at her. "How do you know about them?"

She tapped her temple. "I must've picked up the thought from you. Excuse me for prying."

"The Cylons aren't like the gangs here," he said. "You can't use reason or logic with 'em. But with human-type people, why, I bet you could set up a meeting and work out something. After all, you're all in the same boat, really. Outcasts, living in the City."

"It'll never happen," she assured him.

"Aha, here's the fabled Level 12ES." He rubbed his hands together in anticipation. "Yep, right along the corridor here, Queenie my pet."

She followed him along a dim row of books. "Back on this battlestar where you come from," she asked, "do you have a regular girl?"

"Hum?" He was concentrating on reading the titles on the faded, dusty spines of the books.

"A girl, a steady girl."

"No, nope, not at all," he answered. "That wouldn't be fair. If I committed myself to one lass, all the others would pine and waste away. So I've had to develop the policy of sharing myself with as many of 'em as I. . . . Bingo! A whole row of books about Earth. Damn, I'll just scoop these up and haul 'em back to Apollo. Then we—"

"You ain't," said a new, deep voice behind him.

Slowly, Starbuck turned. "You must be the Commandos," he said.

The black Destroyer ship settled down on the twilight hillside and the gathering darkness seemed to close in around it. After a few silent moments a door near the forward cabin hissed open and a ramp came snaking out.

The pudgy Krebbs was the first to disembark. He was loaded down with gadgets and gear. "I'm picking up indications of life forms nearby, sir," he said after scanning various dials and gauges.

Leiter came down the ramp and stood looking around at the trees that darkly rose up all around the clearing. "How far away?" he asked.

"Less than a mile to the north, Commandent," answered Krebbs.

"We'll take three men with us and leave the other six aboard our Destroyer," the lank Commandent Leiter decided.

"Are we to kill those we encounter, sir?"

"Not immediately," answered Leiter. "First I wish to satisfy my curiosity."

CHAPTER TWENTY–FOUR

There were four of them, and to Starbuck that looked like more than enough. Each of them was big and wide, muscular and shaggy. They wore black trousers and black sleeveless tunics. Each of them carried two large blaster pistols in black leather holsters.

The bigger of the bunch pushed up the bill of his black cap. "Who's this gink, Queenie?"

"He's not part of our gang, Alfie," she said.

"Right, I can see he's too puny for that."

"Hey," put in Starbuck, taking an angry puff of his cigar, "there's no need for personal remarks."

"Haw," said Alfie and his three husky sidekicks echoed the amused sound. "He's a wiseacre, is he?"

"But he's harmless," insisted Queenie as she took protective hold of Starbuck's arm. "I was just escorting him out of the City when—"

"You're forgetting something, Red," cut in Alfie.

"You're forgetting you, the both of you, broke the rules. I mean, this is Commando territory hereabouts."

"Got no right being here," muttered one of the others.

"Since I've always admired you," said Alfie, smiling broadly at the young woman, "I can see to it you get out of this mess alive, more or less. Course, I got to turn you over to the rest of 'em at the clubhouse. Your puny pal here, though, he's finished."

"You never use this library for anything," said the red-haired girl. "So we aren't really hurting—"

"We might, and that ain't the point anyhow, Red," Alfie said with a scowl. "The point is you ain't supposed to be on our territory at all. And another point is we don't want your simp of a pal mucking around in here."

"You guys are going to make me angry if you keep this up," said Starbuck, backing up against the shelf of books he'd been going over. "Let me explain what actually is—"

"Shut your gob," advised Alfie, resting his beefy right hand on the butt of one of his holstered pistols.

"Slice off his ears," suggested one of the other Commandos.

"For a start," added another. "Then we can nail him up to the wall out front, like we done that preacher last—"

"Naw," said Alfie, "that's too tame. For this gink we have to come up with something extra special."

"You're only asking for trouble," warned Queenie. "You hurt him or me and it's only going to make Scrapper mad."

Alfie laughed. "That gink," he said. "He don't scare me no more than this sap you brung along, Red."

"Now you've done it," said Starbuck, taking his burning cigar out of his mouth. "You've made me angry."

Without warning he flipped the cigar right into Alfie's large, flat face.

"Yow!" Sparks flew as it hit him between the eyes.

Starbuck backed quickly into the shelf of books. That was sufficient to topple it, and heavy books came cascading down to hit the other Commandos.

During the diversion Starbuck yanked his captured gun out of Queenie's belt and aimed it at Alfie. He flicked it, swiftly, to a stunning mode and fired.

There was a small humming noise and Alfie stiffened and then fell over on a mound of books.

"Hide behind something," advised Starbuck, grabbing hold of Queenie's hand and pulling her down behind the fallen bookshelves.

The other three Commandos had drawn their pistols and were commencing fire. They weren't interested in stunning, but in killing.

Several books were turned to ashes immediately, books that had been quite close to Starbuck's head.

He risked a look over the top of the shelving and tried a shot.

He missed.

"Might as well give up," said one of the remaining Commandos. "We're going to kill you sooner or later."

"I'd prefer later," said Starbuck.

"We're never going to get free of this," said Queenie as she ducked low.

"Tut tut," said Starbuck, "keep your spirits up. Even when things look darkest there's always—"

"Drop the guns," said a familiar voice. "All six of 'em."

Starbuck counted the thuds that followed. When an even half-dozen pistols had been, reluctantly, dropped to the floor, he stood. "Ah, Captain Apollo himself," he said, grinning. "What an unexpected surprise."

"Where's the redhead?" asked Apollo as he and Cassie set about trussing up the Commandos.

"Right here." Starbuck helped Queenie to her feet. "Queenie, meet Apollo. Also Cassie and Hector and Vector. Feeling better, Hec?"

The android was staying a safe distance from Queenie. "She's the one, Pop. She's the one who put me on the fritz. Miss, I warn you that if you try such a—"

"She's reformed," Starbuck assured him.

"Humdingers! Who ever told you I did any such a—"

"Apollo, listen," said Starbuck, starting to sort through the now scattered books. "I found all sorts of stuff here for us. Books, old chum. With charts, maps, and lord knows what all. All about Earth, also known as Terra. I didn't get to do more than skim a few contents pages before these lunks popped in, but I think when we get this stuff back to the *Galactica*, why, everybody is—"

"That may not be as easy as you think," said Cassie, tying the last knot in the improvised rag rope she'd used to truss up one of the Commandos. "Our ships have been sabotaged."

"Yeah, I heard," said Starbuck. "But, heck, we can fix 'em, can't we?"

Apollo said, "Maybe."

"It's your own darn fault," said Queenie. "Trusting people who you really ought to keep an eye on. You laugh at the way we live here, but at least we—"

"Hush," advised Starbuck.

Apollo picked up one of the books on Earth. "What's the young lady getting at, old buddy?"

"Well, she saw somebody smashing the controls of our vipers."

He dropped the book. "She did? Listen, miss, I need

to find that person because he took some of the parts away with—"

"Wasn't a he," said Queenie with a snort.

"Who was it, then?" Apollo asked.

The red-haired young woman nodded at Starbuck. "Ask him."

Starbuck fished out a fresh cigar and popped it between his teeth. "Queenie thinks she saw a blonde young lady do the deed, Apollo," he said quietly. "Now that might have been Sarah, but on the other hand . . . hell, it could have been some other lady we haven't even met up with yet. Or—"

"I think," said Apollo, "maybe it was Sarah."

Starbuck had the match halfway to the tip of his stogie. "Why would she do that to us? After what we did for her?"

"I'll explain it later," said Apollo. "It's . . . well, in a way I suppose it's my fault."

Vector stepped closer to them. "Might I suggest that we finish up our affairs in this dreadful hole as soon as possible and beat a hasty retreat," he said. "There are no doubt more of these louts lying in wait without."

"At least a dozen," said Queenie. "And all mean as sin."

"Okay," said Starbuck, lighting the new cigar at last. "Soon as I bundle up enough of these books we can push on."

"I'd be glad to carry an armload," said Hector.

Queenie suddenly doubled up and clutched her stomach. "Starbuck," she gasped.

He dashed to her and put an arm around her shoulders. "What's wrong?"

"I'm getting . . . another one of my hunches," she said, face pale and perspiring. "It's . . . it's about that blonde girl we was just talking about."

"Sarah. What about her?"

"She's in . . . trouble," said Queenie. "Real bad trouble."

Night came spilling out of the woodlands. Sarah hugged herself and got up from the lawnchair. "Kids," she announced, "time to get into the house and start cleaning up for dinner."

She could hear all four of them, but she could see only two. They were at the edge of the woods playing a complex and noisy game of hide and seek.

"Kids," she called, louder through cupped hands, "time to quit."

"In a minute," one of them yelled back.

"Now," Sarah said.

Before she could move nearer the woods she heard something behind her.

There were five of them, wearing dark uniforms trimmed with gold-and-dark helmets that hid most of their face. Each wore a holster with a blaster pistol nesting in it and two of them carried blaster rifles.

She recognized the uniform. "It didn't take you long to catch up with us," she said.

A lean man stepped clear of the others, bowed and clicked his heels. "Allow me to introduce myself," he said. "I am Commandent Leiter."

She said nothing.

Leiter smiled thinly. "You are fugitives from Lunar Seven," he said. "At the moment your presence on Paradeen poses no great threat to the Alliance. What you do from now on is of little interest to me."

Sarah took a step back from him. "Then what do you want?"

Stroking the scar on his cheek, the commandent said,

"You were accompanied here by two other ships. I wish to know about them."

She shook her head. "I don't know a thing," she told him. "Nothing at all."

Leiter lunged and caught her arm, gripping it tightly. "Listen to me, young woman," he said in a low voice. "You have children to consider. It is, of course, distasteful to me to torture young people. I shall, however, do so unless you cooperate fully. Is that perfectly clear?"

"Yes." She nodded once and then kicked him in the knee as hard as she could. Wrenching free of his grip, Sarah turned and called out to the children. "Run! Get away from here! Run, quick!"

Leiter, limping, came after the blonde young woman and caught her. "Very foolish." He caught her left arm and twisted it up behind her back. "Very foolish. Slepyan, go after those damned children. Bring back as many as you can."

Saluting, the husky Slepyan asked, "Alive, sir?"

"Yes, alive," said Leiter. "You and I, young woman, will step into the house over there and have a talk. Krebbs, make certain there's no one else inside that place."

"All my gear indicates that there isn't any—"

"Doublecheck it," said the commandent.

As he escorted Sarah toward the house she could hear the children running away through the dark woods.

And she could hear the man with the blaster rifle going after them.

CHAPTER TWENTY–FIVE

Cindy fell.

Her foot caught in a twist of root and the blonde little girl went sprawling. She didn't cry out, knowing it was dangerous to make noise, and so none of the other fleeing children knew she was down. Cindy had been bringing up the rear.

Her ankle was commencing to hurt. She got to her knees, struggling not to sob. Pain was throbbing in her leg.

Darkness stretched out all around her and the trunks of the trees looked like rows of enormous bars meant to lock her in.

Pushing her hands against the mossy ground, Cindy was able to rise to her feet. She found she could walk, although her ankle hurt an awful lot. Running was impossible, but she'd keep walking and she'd catch up with the other kids soon. Maybe.

She'd taken only a few shaky steps when she became aware of heavy footfalls behind her. She didn't look back but kept hobbling along.

"Stop, please, little girl," ordered a gruff voice.

Cindy kept walking.

"I don't want to use the stunner on you," said the uniformed man who'd caught up with her. "I will, though, unless you halt at once."

Starting to cry quietly, the little girl stopped and turned to face him.

He looked immense. Like part of the night in his dark uniform and helmet. The silvery rifle seemed to float in the night, pointing down at her.

"Where are the others?" he asked, crouching.

Cindy kept on crying, a fist to the corner of one eye.

"Where are they?" he repeated.

"Don't know."

"I think you do," he said, extending the gun until the barrel touched her small chest. "Yes, you must have hiding places in these woods. So you tell me, quick now."

"Don't know," the child insisted.

"You don't want me to hurt you? There's no need for that, is there?" The tip of the barrel began to dig into her flesh.

"Don't know," she said yet again.

"Listen to me, you tell me where they're hiding or.... Wow!"

All at once his rifle left his hands and went soaring away up into the dark tangle of branches high overhead.

Making a surprised gulping noise, he jumped to his feet and snatched out his pistol.

That, too, left his hand.

It went spinning off into the darkness.

"Who did that?" he demanded. "Little girl, how did you.... Hey!"

Now he himself was flying. His big feet left the ground and he rose up at an increasing speed. He leveled off and his skull began to bang against the trunk of a thick tree. He howled and protested, but he couldn't stop himself from battering the bole with his head. In less than five minutes he was out cold and then he drifted down to settle in a heap near the puzzled little girl's feet.

"Well, sir, that takes care of him. Poking little girls with guns, eh?" A bearded old man appeared from behind the trunk of one of the trees and smiled at Cindy. "We took care of him."

She asked, "How?"

"Oh, it's a little knack I have."

"I don't know you," Cindy informed him.

"That's right. I haven't gotten around to introducing myself to you and your friends." He held out his hand. "I'm known as Kurtiz the Hermit in these parts."

"What are you known as in other parts?"

He stroked his scraggly beard and thought about that. "I don't imagine I'm known at all. What's your name?"

"Cindy. Can you take me home?"

Kurtiz said, "I think it's best to get you settled safely elsewhere for the nonce. Let me tie this dumbbell up and then we'll find your friends and see you get put up somewhere. Is that okay with you?"

"Can I ever go home?"

"Soon," promised the hermit.

Leiter stood with his narrow back to the fireplace. His helmet sat on a nearby table, catching the scarlet glow of the blaze and reflecting it. "Slepyan will be back soon," he said.

"Perhaps." Sarah sat, arms folded, on the edge of the armchair.

"Meaning exactly what, my dear?"

"Oh, that perhaps there are some things on this planet you don't know about," she replied. "Things in the woods that might . . . delay your man."

Leiter chuckled. "I doubt that."

"There might even be things out there that'll take care of the guards you have stationed around my house."

"Oh, yes, to be sure," said the commandant. "I see. You're hoping that your friends will return and overcome my men." He shook his head. "That is highly unlikely, since every man aboard the Destroyer is a most efficient fighter."

"Then you've nothing to worry about."

"Nothing, no," he agreed. He rubbed his hands together a few times, watching her. "You can save us all a good deal of trouble, my dear, if you'll tell me now what I want to know. I actually mean your children no harm."

"How many children have you killed so far in your career, Commandant? When you bomb cities and—"

"Those aren't children, they're statistics merely," he said with a bleak smile. "Where did those other two ships come from? Who was aboard?"

"I have no idea."

"But you do," he said, growing angry. "I know they escorted your ship here. The ships are not from Lunar Seven or any other known planet."

"Makes for quite a puzzle, doesn't it?"

He strode across the room and took hold of both of her shoulders. "Tell me," he shouted, shaking her.

Sarah made no reply at all.

Leiter made an angry growling noise and threw her back down into the chair. "You're being a fool, nothing more," he said as he walked back to the fire. "Sooner or later we'll capture not only your children but all the others as well. If you . . . yes, what is it?"

The door had opened and a uniformed man came into the room. He saluted, hand ticking smartly against his dark helmet.

Leiter's eyes narrowed. "I instructed you to stay outside and stand watch," he said.

"Something's come up, sir." The uniformed man marched into the room.

Two more followed him in out of the darkness.

The commandent said, "What's going on, you idiots? You can't all abandon your duties to—"

"Oh, but this is very important," said another of the guards, puffing on his cigar.

Leiter started walking toward him. "Why are you smoking on duty?"

"Well, the kind of duties I have call for a little diversion now and then, old chum." He drew a pistol from his holster and pointed it at the commandent. "Now, I suggest you put your hands up high."

"What?"

Starbuck removed the borrowed helmet and grinned at the perplexed Commandent Leiter. "Your boys are slumbering out on the grass," he explained. "We . . . well, we took advantage of 'em, I fear. Snuck up and decked the whole set before they even knew what hit 'em. Hardly sporting, but very effective. Now we have you, too."

Leiter tried a confident laugh. "I still have several highly efficient men aboard my ship," he said, drawing himself up straight. "When we don't return by a given time, they'll storm this place and whip the lot of you from—"

"You're using the wrong tense, old buddy," Apollo told him as he got out of his helmet. "You *had* a crew."

Exhaling smoke, Starbuck said, "We paid them a surprise visit before dropping in here."

"I don't believe—"

"Believe it or not," said Starbuck, grin widening, "you've lost this round, Commandent."

Michael was the last to take off the enemy helmet. Doing so, he moved to the young woman's side. "Sarah, are you all right?"

She reached up and took his hand. "Yes, I'm fine," she said, standing. "But the kids, they ran off in the forest when these people arrived. We'll have to find them."

He nodded. "We'll do that now," he said.

Starbuck, gun still aimed at the defeated commandent, eased nearer to the fire. "Apollo, old chum," he said. "I was thinking about that Destroyer ship these lads travel in."

"So was I," he answered. "Roomy, isn't it?"

"Yep, the decor is a little grim, but it would fit all of us nicely inside," said Starbuck, warming his backside at the crackling fire. "Why don't we, since our ships are on the fritz, borrow the darn thing?"

"An excellent notion," said Apollo.

They met them in the forest.

Michael sensed their approach first and put a restraining arm up to halt Sarah. "People coming," he warned, drawing his pistol.

"Maybe it's the children coming—"

"No, these are adults."

Three men came into view, each carrying a rifle. They slowed when they spotted Michael and Sarah on the dark path.

"We're coming to help you," said one of the men. "My name's Sut Meadows. We're sort of neighbors."

"If you don't want our help, just say so," another of them said. "I still think we ought to mind our own business, but Annie, my wife, insists we—"

"Mr. Moreland here," explained Sut, "ain't nowhere as mean and ornery as he acts. Neither is his cousin Rick."

Rick was a hefty blond young man. He gave them a tentative smile and said, "Howdy."

Sarah took a few steps toward them. "We're hunting for the children. Have you—"

"Course we have," said Joshua Moreland. "That's how come we're here."

"They're all safe and sound," said Sut, grinning. "At the Moreland spread, being looked after by Mrs. Moreland. They showed up there and told about how you'd been busted in on by Alliance troops."

"Where are they?" asked Moreland. "We decided we'd best fight 'em this time. Before they come busting in on all of us."

"Right," agreed Rick.

Michael said, "We appreciate your offer of help. Fortunately, they've been taken care of."

Sut snapped his fingers. "I bet I know how, too," he said. "It was them other outlanders. That Apollo feller and his buddies. Weren't it?"

"It was," answered Sarah. "Now can you take us to the children? I want them to know we're all right."

"Sure, come on along," invited Moreland. "You might as well see where we live, since we're going to be stuck with each other as neighbors, I reckon. Until the Alliance strikes again, anyhow."

Michael said, "It's just possible the Alliance is going to be leaving us alone from now on, Mr. Moreland."

"Might as well call me Josh," he said. "How you mean?"

Sarah said, "Our friends have thrown quite a scare into them. And I don't think they're through with them yet."

Moreland spit into the brush. "Remains to be seen," he said. "But for now we might as well try to get along."

"A good idea," said Michael, holding out his hand.

Sut nudged Moreland. "Shake hands, you stubborn nitwit."

Moreland held out his hand. "We'll see how being friendly goes," he said.

CHAPTER TWENTY–SIX

The morning of departure was chill and grey.

Sarah shivered slightly as she and Apollo stood looking at the Destroyer ship some thousand yards uphill. "I will miss you," she said softly.

"I know," he said. "Someday, maybe, we'll see each other again."

"No." She shook her head. "This is the last time."

"I think you'll be able to have a pretty good life here on Paradeen now."

"Yes, I suppose," she said. "We have new friends and . . . well, eventually Michael and I may like each other a good deal more than we do now."

"Seems to me he's pretty fond of you right now, Sarah."

She looked away, toward the forest. "There's one last thing I have to talk about with you, Apollo."

He reached out and put his hand on her shoulder. "I

know what you're going to tell me," he said.

"About who smashed your ships?"

"Yes, I knew you'd done it," he said.

"It was such an awful thing to do," she said, "so mean and stupid."

"I understand why, Sarah," he said. "You wanted us to stay and when persuasion didn't work, you took a drastic step."

"I was so angry," she said. "At you, at Michael, at this whole damn planet. My father was dead and you were deserting me, too."

"Most of us lose control a few times in our lives," he said. "At least you didn't strand us on Paradeen. The Destroyer came along at just the right time."

"But if it hadn't—"

"Oh, Starbuck and I would've been able to patch at least one ship and get back to the *Galactica* for help."

"You think I'm just a spoiled child, not a woman. I can tell by the tone of your voice."

"You acted on impulse," Apollo said. "I don't much admire what you did, Sarah, but I understand why. And as for your being a child. . . ."

Gently, he turned her to face him. Leaning, he kissed her once.

Starbuck hurried along the dark corridor of the Destroyer, blowing cigar smoke up toward the strutted ceiling. "*Galactica*, here I come," he was singing to himself.

"Hey!"

He slowed as a door opened beside him. "Ah, my favorite passenger and the unofficial mascot of the whole—"

"Humdingers! Will you stop babbling, Starbuck, and let a person get a word in," requested Queenie, who had her red hair braided and was clad in a suit of workclothes. "I want to talk to you."

"I'm enroute to the bridge to consult with Apollo," he told her. "According to my calculations, child, we ought to be nearing the *Galactica* after many long and weary days in space aboard this flying mortuary of a ship."

"Well, dang, that's exactly what I mean to talk about," the girl said, leaning in the doorway of her cabin.

Starbuck smote the side of his head. "Now don't go telling me you're sorry you came and want to be hauled back home to Paradeen."

"Paradeen you can stuff in your nose," she said. "What I'm fretful about, Starbuck, is this here battlestar of yours."

"Queenie, they're going to love you on the battlestar," he assured the worried young woman. "I can name you a dozen gents who'll fall at your feet in awe. Besides me there's an ample chap name of Jolly and Chavez and—"

"Hush," she requested, touching his hand. "You can sweet talk me all you want, but I know what I am."

"You're a cute little redhead with all sorts of talents, wild and otherwise. What the heck is wrong with that?"

"I'm just a girl who ran with a gang in the ruins of the City," she said. "They'll all know that when they see me. I mean, your friend Cassie is so . . . well, she's a lady."

Starbuck laughed. "So are you," he said.

"They'll laugh at me, make fun."

He leaned close to her. "Listen, pet," he said. "Everybody gets a certain amount of razzing when he or she goes into a new situation. Heck, now and then even someone as flawless as yours truly gets kidded. What you have to do is ignore it."

"Easy to say, but—"

"I will guarantee that within a couple of months on the *Galactica* you'll be one of the gang," he said. "One of the *Galactica* gang, that is. Just remember, you're pretty and smart . . . and, listen, most everybody is going to fall under the spell of that red hair."

"I surely hope so."

He kissed her on the cheek. "Be of stout heart, Queenie," he said. "With Starbuck as your champion no harm can befall you."

"Okay," she said, smiling hopefully and stepping back inside her cabin.

Grinning, Starbuck continued on his way.

He found Apollo on the bridge along with Cassie and two of the Destroyer's original crew. Commandent Leiter was also present, sitting stiffly in a chair.

"Ah," said Starbuck, puffing on his cigar as he came across the room, "just think. In a short time I'll be snoozing in my own little bed again."

"Yeah, we're getting close to the *Galactica*," said Apollo, who was standing near a scanner screen.

"Course, I won't get much time for sleep," said the grinning lieutenant, "since the folks'll be carrying me around on their shoulders and feting me in various ways. Bringing home all this information on Earth, that's quite an achievement. That library on Paradeen was sure a find."

"We've got a heck of a lot more information than we had," agreed Apollo.

"The only thing that's worrying me," said Starbuck, "is how I'm going to return those books. I'd hate to have an overdue charge slapped on me."

"Fool," said Leiter under his breath.

Starbuck cupped his ear. "Eh?"

"All of you are fools," said the commandent in a

louder voice. "You've gotten this far, but your day will come. You fail to realize that we have the most advanced military force in the galaxy."

"So you've been saying," said Apollo.

"Retribution will be swift once it's learned that you've had the audacity to—"

"Commandent," cut in Apollo, gesturing at the screen. "I had you brought here from your quarters for a reason. You—"

"Quarters? I don't consider the brig fitting quarters for an officer of my rank. Further, I intend to lodge a formal—"

"Pay attention to what we're trying to show you," said Starbuck. "I really think it'll change your outlook."

"Nonsense. I. . . ." He leaned forward in his seat, staring now at the screen. "Good lord, what is that?"

On the screen showed the Battlestar *Galactica*.

"It's our home ship," said Apollo. "We'll be docking there in a matter of hours."

Leiter ran his tongue over his dry lips. "I . . . I've never seen anything as big as that. Never. . . ."

Apollo folded his arms and looked full at the commandent. "What was that you were telling us about this invincible Alliance of yours?" he asked.

There was no immediate answer.